Bird
Face

Port
Yonder
Press

Bird Face

Cynthia T. Toney

Linda,
For extraordinary support,
thank you so much.
Cynthia Toney

All rights reserved. Published by SharksFinn Books, an imprint of Port Yonder Press, LLC. Publisher since 2009. This is a work of fiction. All persons appearing in this work are fictitious. Any resemblance to real people, living or dead, is entirely coincidental.

Edited by Chila Woychik
Editorial assistance provided by Linda Yezak
Other readers: Heidi Kortman, Lisa Cantrell, Lisa Lickel

www.PortYonderPress.com

ISBN 9781935600435
Library of Congress Control Number 2012949650

Book design by behindthegift.com

First paperback edition, 2014

Printed in the U.S.A.

To my parents, Nick and Carolyn, who did not survive to see this book or other products of my heart and soul reach maturity, and to Abby, who is the best of those products.

One

Nice face, the yellow sticky-note read.

Sarcasm. Wasn't that the lowest form of wit?

I returned the note to my back pocket and began folding bath towels.

There were worse things than an ugly face. Like being stuck at home on Saturday morning. And much more, I'd soon learn.

"Wendy, don't forget!" Mom's voice spanned the house from end to end.

Blood rushed to my cheeks, and my head pounded. *Cut me some slack, would you?* No wonder Daddy left us. *God, I didn't mean that.* I loved my mother—I just hated that she got to lie in bed on Saturday morning recovering from surgery while I hurried to do all the chores. Carpal tunnel syndrome. Her job caused the problem, but I suffered the consequences. And I wanted to get over to Jennifer's house, like *now*, to show her the note.

A week's worth of bath towels folded in under a minute—a new record. But instead of checking "Fold towels" on the chore list, I poked a hole in the paper with my pencil. *Rrrip.* The paper tore on the upstroke, while the pencil point broke off and flew who-knows-where. I growled and lifted the stack of towels.

"Wendy, did you hear me?"

I blew air through my teeth like pressure out of a tire. "Don't worry, your sheets are on my list." I dug my chin into the tower of towels to keep it from swaying out of control as I carried it from the laundry room.

"There's old dead skin in my bed, you know."

I pictured a snake wriggling out of its skin and leaving it behind in one piece, like I'd seen on one of the nature channels. What a drama queen. Ever since she read that our bodies lose skin cells in our beds each night, she obsessed about those sheets. I would've rolled my eyes, but it was hard enough to watch where I was going.

When I made a sharp turn into the living room, something hooked the ragged corner of a towel—the beak of a giant glass parrot rescued in one of Mom's roadside scavenger hunts. Its head extended beyond the sofa table's edge.

"Oh…!" I clamped my lips together, having made a promise to Father Gerard at my last confession not to cuss. I stuck my hand out just in time and prevented the rainbow-colored monstrosity from toppling over.

Mom now stood in the opening between the hallway and

living room. She nodded in the direction of the parrot. "That's probably one of a kind."

How about *embarrassing piece of junk*. Like almost everything in our house. Once covered in somebody else's dust and grime, it now made up part of what she called our *décor*. I couldn't wait until I graduated from high school and got my own place. Everything would be brand new.

After dropping the towels onto the bathroom counter, I ran to Mom's room to strip her bed. Better go ahead and get it over with. There would be plenty left to do when I got back from Jennifer's. I pulled back the antique quilt and threw it to the floor, then yanked the sheets off the mattress.

Why couldn't I have an older brother? He would help me with the heavy chores, plus watch out for me. We could hang around together, and Mom wouldn't be so lonely for Dad. He would look a lot like me, with brown hair and brown eyes, but taller and…

Mom shuffled toward the kitchen wearing her ratty old bathrobe with the fuzzy pink flowers. She would want her coffee.

I started the washing machine and caught up with her in her favorite spot at the kitchen table. She studied the splint on her right wrist and the soft brace on her left. I poured a mug of coffee and placed it in front of her. "What would you like for breakfast?"

She smiled. "Just some scrambled eggs and toast. Thanks, sweetie."

"After we eat, can I go on over to Jen's?" I dropped some

whole wheat slices into the toaster and cracked four eggs into the skillet.

"Sure, if you call first and make sure it's all right with her parents. And—"

"I know, Mom. Call you when I get there." What did she think? I'd be abducted by aliens? I was almost fourteen years old, for heaven's sake.

Her gaze relaxed and turned toward her coffee. She wrapped the five swollen fingers of her left hand around the mug handle and took a sip. "The toast smells like it's ready."

I manually popped up the toast as the first crumbs began to burn, then set a plate of scrambled eggs and toast on the table.

She curled the fingers of her right hand around her fork and lifted a piece of egg to her mouth as though it weighed a hundred pounds.

I tried to ignore how pitiful she looked while I shoveled in a few bites of egg without tasting them and gulped down a small glass of orange juice.

"Slow down before you choke. Jennifer can wait an extra five minutes." Translation: *Stay and eat breakfast with me.*

I slowed down only a little and cleared away my dishes before Mom finished. With a quick phone call, I got permission from Jennifer's father.

"Give me a hug." Mom reached out her arms.

I hugged her goodbye and bolted for the back door.

"Maybe we'll order pizza for dinner. Be home before dark." Her volume control went up a notch on each word of her last sentence.

I let the door slam behind me.

An April morning in Louisiana waited outside, one as perfect as it gets for riding a bike on the curving streets of Maywood Hills. Clear and sunny, but only warm enough to keep the goose bumps away. Rain had washed most of the pollen from cars and patio covers where it had collected the week before, leaving little dried-up rivers of yellow on the ground. A cool breeze tickled my nose. The air never smelled so clean.

Freedom. I swung my leg over the seat of my dark blue Schwinn, a joint Christmas gift from Mom and Dad.

My new sports bra—the smallest one I could find in the store—was still a little stiff and scratchy against my chest, but beat-up Reeboks more than made up for that discomfort. I pulled my ponytail from beneath the collar of my windbreaker and zipped it halfway up. Better zip all the way up for the ride. Rats! The zipper's teeth caught my t-shirt. A thrift store find. "Never Underestimate the Power of a Woman," it read. I twisted my mouth to the left and struggled with the zipper. Man, it was really stuck. Whatever. I'd have to deal with it later.

I released the kickstand and pushed forward. Was my front tire going flat? If that squishy black ring beyond my khaki shorts and bony winter-white legs was any indication, yeah, it could use a pump or two of air. Forget it. I was running late enough already.

I took off down the cracked driveway with clothing pressed against the front of my body like shrink-wrap. Scrawny leg muscles worked to put as much distance between me and my life as possible.

One back pocket held the note. The other carried the guilt.

I shot like a rocket up the street, headed toward Jennifer's house. Cars and trucks parked in driveways and along the curb reflected my funhouse-mirror image. My head stretched and shrank, eyeballs drooped and then disappeared, nose ballooned out. I was a monster—a girl who abandoned her mother. My heart and stomach swapped places. Was I like my father? Someone who put his personal happiness ahead of his own family? I *couldn't* be like him.

I squeezed my eyes shut for a second and shook my head to rearrange my thoughts. I had to see Jennifer. She would make everything better.

My spirits lifted as I turned the corner into the newer section of Maywood Hills. Houses grew taller and wider, with fresh paint and roofs without patches or missing shingles. Green front lawns called out to children to lie down in the grass and lose themselves in cotton-puff clouds playing in the sky.

Half a block away, Jennifer sat cross-legged on the sidewalk near her mailbox, her golden hair gleaming in the sunlight.

I glanced at my watch. Yes! Another record broken. Less than five minutes from my driveway to Jennifer's house, in spite of a low tire. I smiled to myself and pulled off the street.

Jennifer leapt to her feet and ran to meet me in the driveway as soon as I started slowing down. I coasted my bike up to her.

"Wait 'til you see," she said before I had a chance to stop and reach into my pocket. Her cheeks glowed a healthy pink through a scattering of freckles.

"What is it?" I slid off the seat and lowered the kickstand.

She pressed her lips together as if to keep a juicy secret from spilling out. Her hand locked onto mine, and she dragged me around the side of the house to the back yard. "Look."

Five tiny puppies lay in the grass near the wall. Turned every which-way with heads, legs, and tails overlapping one another, they slept against their mother's belly. Two of the puppies were black, one was brown, one was yellow like its mother, and the last was honey-colored.

My insides melted. "Oh-h-h," I whispered. "Where did you get them?"

"We heard crying last night and found them back here. My dad said somebody might have dropped them off, or maybe the mother dog moved them here to protect them."

Mr. Sampson walked up and stood beside us. "What do you think, Wendy Robichaud?" He pronounced my last name with a funny French accent, like Inspector Clouseau of those old Pink Panther movies. It didn't really sound Cajun like my dad's relatives, but that was okay.

"They're so cute." I could barely take my eyes off the puppies long enough to acknowledge him.

"Can we keep one, pl-e-e-ease?" Jennifer begged her father—not for the first time, I was sure. Only five months difference in our ages but she could be such a baby sometimes.

"Well, we'll keep them all for now, at least." Mr. Sampson patted and squeezed Jennifer's shoulder. "They need to stay with their mother until they get a little bigger."

Jennifer grinned and squealed and bounced on her toes.

"They'll take a lot of work, though." Mr. Sampson raised his brows at us. "And someone will have to find permanent homes for them eventually."

My heart still ached from the memory of my dog, Angel. I'd found her fluffy white body lying next to a pair of Dad's old shoes after he'd moved out. Could a dog die of grief? No dog deserved to be abandoned by someone it loved. This dog and her puppies needed a second chance at happiness. Maybe Jennifer and I could give that to them.

I'd have to work something out with Mom, and that could be a challenge. Let's see, if I got off the bus at three thirty and took about an hour and a half to do chores and help fix dinner, another hour and a half for homework, a half hour for television, and a half hour to get ready for bed, that would leave an hour and a half I could use for the puppies. A tight schedule, but doable if Mom cooperated. "I'll help." I nodded like a bobblehead. "I can come over every day after school."

Mr. Sampson smiled. "*Chienne chanceaux*—she's a lucky dog," he said, and the name stuck.

I borrowed Mr. Sampson's cell phone to call Mom. Then Jennifer and I got to work. We cut an opening in one side of a cardboard box and used an old blanket Mr. Sampson found in the attic to make a soft bed. We placed the bed by the back door of the covered patio and filled a bowl with water and a pie pan with dry dog food Mrs. Sampson had purchased.

Chanceaux watched our every move, her big brown eyes flitting between her puppies and us. Jennifer and I spoke in soft voices and were careful not to make much noise.

Mrs. Sampson slid the patio door open. "I thought you girls might need some help moving them."

"Do you think Chanceaux will let us?" I asked. The puppies had finished nursing and fallen asleep again.

"I think she understands we won't hurt her babies. Let's try." She patted the blanket with one hand. "Come on, girl."

Chanceaux looked at her, eyed the blanket, and walked over to her new bed.

We carried the puppies one at a time and placed them next to their mother. The last one I picked up was my favorite, the honey-colored runt of the litter. I stroked her velvet ears against my cheek and inhaled her sweet, milky puppy-breath. Her eyes weren't open yet, but I could tell she liked me.

With the puppies settled in place, I dusted my hands on the back of my shorts.

Oh, yeah—the note. "Jen, let's go inside. There's something I need to show you."

The inside of Jennifer's house was like a beautiful banquet, and every part of me craved what it offered. I ran my hand over the back of a buttery-soft, white leather chair. My soul drank in the colorful modern paintings framed in chrome that hung above the matching sofa. My eyes gobbled up the glazed pottery and shiny silver objects resting on dark wood tables polished to a high gloss. Nothing was stale or dusty or musty like at my house. I took a deep breath, inhaling delicious smells of clean, of fresh, of never-been-used-before.

When we reached Jennifer's room, I closed the door behind us. I pulled the note from my pocket and handed it to her. "Look what somebody wrote to me."

"Hmm." Jennifer held the note in her right hand and placed her left index finger against her cheek.

"So what do you think?"

"Wait a minute." She walked over to her desk and picked up a magnifying glass.

"Just tell me!" Laughing, I grabbed a lace-trimmed throw pillow off the bed and fired it at her.

She dodged the pillow without taking her eyes off the piece of paper. "'Nice face,'" she read aloud, adding, "No signature." Her blonde brows pinched together above her nose.

"Right," I said, "and it's printed instead of script."

"It seems like they would have said 'You have a nice face' or 'I like your face.'" She turned the note over and checked the other side. "'Nice face' sounds a little weird."

"Or sarcastic, depending on how you look at it."

She shrugged. "Maybe it's meant to be a compliment from somebody who likes you."

"Well, if that's the case, it would've been nice if he—if it is a *he*—had asked me to the Spring Dance. His timing stinks. I had to stay home last Saturday night like the rest of the losers."

"*I* didn't go." She placed her free hand on her hip. "And I was with you."

"But you could have gone. Any boy at school would've flipped if you'd asked him."

She rolled her eyes. "Just forget about that."

"Okay, okay." I obviously wasn't going to get any sympathy. She handed the note back to me. "So, where'd you find it?"

"Stuck inside the cover of my history book."

"Then maybe it's from somebody in history class."

"Maybe, but the book sat on top of my backpack in the bus line after school yesterday."

"Then it could be from almost anybody."

This was getting me nowhere. I lowered my chin and looked up at her from beneath my brows. "I *know*."

Jennifer's blue eyes sparkled. "You should start searching for clues."

Yeah, like I needed another project. "But really, do you think it's from a girl—or a boy?"

"Because the letters are so blocky, my guess is a boy." She gave a single nod in confirmation of her decision and rummaged through a shopping bag on the floor.

I couldn't argue. Jennifer had proven herself the better authority on the subject of boys often enough. For sure, boys paid more attention to Jennifer than to me, and she didn't even have to make an effort. She had the start of a great body and was the natural kind of pretty. Not the Tookie Miller kind that scraped off and left a white spot if she scratched her face.

"Good, I found it." Jennifer pulled her iPod out of the bag. "I downloaded some MP3s."

While she docked the iPod on her speakers, I went straight to the chamber of fascination otherwise known as Jennifer's closet. So much clothing crammed in there. Little strips of color like in a Vincent van Gogh painting. "Bought anything lately?" I poked around in the overflowing junior-sized fashions. Without meaning to, I knocked one end of a hanger out of a blouse. The blouse stayed in place, squeezed between the others like it was glued there. "Sorry."

"Ha!" Jennifer bellowed. "That happens all the time."

Like a magician performing a scarf trick, she reached in and whipped out two new outfits. "Now, this blue and white-striped button-down casual shirt looks great with these khaki pants." She held the first outfit against her front. "And this red knit top with the bow on the neckline works with this black satin skirt because it's not orangey-red. That would be too Halloween-y."

I laughed but nodded. Jennifer acted so serious when coordinating her wardrobe.

"Want to borrow?" She began re-hanging the items.

None of Jennifer's clothes looked as comfortable as the t-shirts and shorts I liked for spring. "No thanks, I'm good for now. My mom and I hit the after-Easter sales."

"Okay." Jennifer started at one end of the closet and reviewed piece by piece until Mrs. Sampson tapped on the door and saved me.

"Lunch."

"Thanks, Mom." Jennifer took the tray of sandwiches, potato chips, and sodas from her hands.

We climbed onto Jennifer's mountain of a bed and ate under its pink and white ruffled canopy while we listened to Katy Perry. I preferred Taylor Swift, but that was okay. True friendship must have give-and-take like that.

"Oh, I almost forgot." Jennifer rolled over from where we lay side by side across her comforter, drowsy from lunch. She sat straight up.

I reluctantly lifted my head from the down-filled coziness and propped up on my elbows.

"You're not going to believe what I'm getting." Her eyes grew big and round.

"What?"

"A makeover."

The words hit me like a punch to the stomach. Maybe by a two-year-old, but still, it didn't feel good. I sat straight up too and blinked once, hard. In front of me were Jennifer's long blonde hair, little turned-up nose, and perfect complexion that didn't even need makeup. If anybody needed a makeover, it was me. I could've used a make*over-haul*.

Jennifer waited, staring at me.

I reminded myself that I was her best friend. "When?" I forced a smile.

"Next Saturday. My mom's treating herself to one for her birthday, and she's letting me have one too. We're going to the salon at the mall. Isn't that great?"

"Yeah. I can't wait to see what they do to you." My enthusiasm sounded real enough. To me, anyway.

"I'll come over afterward and show you."

"Promise?" I asked.

"Promise." She raised her right hand, with the first three fingers upright and her thumb holding down her bent pinkie. The Girl Scout sign.

The rest of the afternoon passed like a flash. It always did when we were together.

As I rode my bike home at dusk, I tried to be happy for Jennifer about her makeover. I really wanted to be. But she already had everything—a great house, great clothes, great parents, and good looks too.

An unfamiliar thought entered my mind: Why did everything good have to happen to Jennifer instead of me? I tried to shove the thought aside. It stayed. I gritted my teeth and rode faster, hoping to leave the idea behind me on the street. I had to dodge a basketball and almost lost control of the bike. The thought was still there. What was that commandment? Thou shalt not covet thy neighbor's...life. I repeated the commandment to myself all the way home. But envy continued to build as I left Jennifer's world and returned to my own.

TWO

What could I say about Bellingrath Junior High? Not much, except it was named after my secret hero, Bernard Bellingrath. But Barney wasn't the kind of hero who rescued a kid from a burning building or found a cure for a disease.

Barney dropped a big load of money on our school to build the gym, stadium, and later the library annex. As his reward, a faded portrait hung on the wall of the visitors' area inside the main entrance. But that wasn't the reason he was my hero.

According to legend, Barney had been born with a tail. A *tail*. Grand-mere Robichaud, who'd once seen such a tail on a baby's pink bottom, said he could've been mistaken for the main course at a *cochon de lait*—a Cajun pig roast. But Barney's parents were very religious, so they refused to have the tail removed.

In spite of that decision, Barney grew up to be the richest and most powerful man in town. But that still wasn't the reason he

was my hero. The fact that he decided to keep the tail anyway—
that was the reason.

Now, all these years later, you'd think physical imperfections
would be tolerated at a school practically *founded* by someone
with a tail. But no.

Our bus pulled into the line of yellow-orange behemoths and
braked to a screeching halt that made my teeth hurt. I tucked my
gold crucifix and chain, inherited from Grand-mere, inside my
shirt and out of sight. My wad of gum dropped from my mouth
into a piece of notebook paper and then into my purse.

Outside my bus window, groups of students stood around on
the front lawn. I carefully avoided making eye contact with any
of them. You could lose an arm for doing that.

*Ladies and gentlemen, please pay close attention while on
safari and keep your heads and hands inside the windows at all
times.*

*Observe the small group of Brainiacs sitting together on a
cement bench along the central walkway. Brainiacs are super
smart and make perfect scores on nearly every test. They dress
alike, talk alike, and huddle in their herds. Yet they yearn to be
accepted by the other animals, while hoping not to be eaten by
any of them.*

*Notice the huge oak tree to your right, where the Sticks
gather in a conversational cluster, shunning females from the
other groups. Examine, if you will, this clique of girls who*

strive to be as skinny as possible to maintain what they think is a fashionable figure. The only thing heavy about them is their makeup. Tookie Miller is their leader and the skinniest of them all. See her long skinny hair? It is the symbol of her dominance, and no other member of the herd is allowed to grow her hair longer than Tookie's. To maximize their lean look, the Sticks wear the highest heels or platform shoes allowed by the dress code. They do so because they have no desire to travel great distances in search of food.

Near the Sticks you will find the Suaves, and the two exist in a symbiotic relationship to make each other look good. Can you spot a few Suaves leaning against the oak tree in model-like poses? Suaves have parents with enough money for their sons to show off the latest hairstyles and designer clothing but apparently not enough to send them to private schools.

On the steps outside the front door—

"All right, everybody out." The bus driver half-turned toward his cargo and slid the toothpick between his lips from one side to the other with his tongue.

The doors whooshed open.

Jennifer finished talking to a seventh-grade girl sitting behind us. I grabbed my backpack, took a deep breath, and rose from my seat. What abuse awaited me today?

A boy's voice drifted from the back of the bus. "Hey, girl, there're some strings hanging down from your skirt."

I twisted around to check.

"Ouch. I'm sorry, those are your legs," he added, followed by a loud hoot.

Beads of sweat erupted above my lip. *Let me out of here.* But the aisle was blocked with kids.

Jennifer spun so fast her hair slapped me in the face. "Have you looked in a mirror lately?" she asked the troublemaker. She placed a hand on her hip, cocked her head, and raised one eyebrow at him.

The boy's face got as red as a boiled crawfish, and his friends snickered and shoved him.

I waited until we stepped down from the bus and then said, "I owe you one."

Jennifer waved my debt away. "It was nothing."

Nothing to Jennifer, but something I wished I could have done for myself.

Squatting in front of my bottom-row locker, I tried to avoid the crotch view of a fellow student above me. I loaded my arms with books for morning classes, my knees straining under the weight.

I glanced to my left, past a dirty gym sock, three lost pencils, and a ball of hair from somebody's brush. A few feet away, Gayle Freeman, girl Brainiac, sat cross-legged on the floor in front of her locker, her eyeglasses fogged from peering so deeply into it. Brown legs peeked from beneath a skirt that wouldn't have made the Sticks' approved fashion list. No makeup, boring hair held with barrettes, and a wad of gum stuck to the bottom of her scuffed shoe. Next to her, Frank Chawlk rested on his knees, digging through his books like a raccoon in a trashcan. A complexion like he'd spent a year in solitary confinement. He pushed against his locker door with both hands, trying to close it, but didn't realize that a notebook was stuck between the hinges.

My back stiffened as the thought hit me: Not a single popular student was at the bottom. Not one! There never had been. No way were locker assignments "random" like the orientation brochure stated. Three years at this school, and I just noticed that?

At the next bank of lockers to my right, Tookie stood between a Stick and a Suave. Chatting while selecting their books, the three of them were the picture of perfection. Perfect hair, perfect makeup, perfect clothes.

I gave them my meanest evil eye, the Cajun one Grand-mere Robichaud taught me. An eyelash came loose and poked me in the eyeball. *Dang it!* And no free hand to brush it away. I blew air toward it from the corner of my mouth. No good. The best thing to do was keep the eye closed or risk upsetting the delicate balance of books in my arms. I grunted, straightened my knees, and rose to my feet.

I struggled down the hall until I couldn't stand it any longer, then withdrew an arm from under the weight and reached for my eye.

All but the last book slid out of my grasp and onto the floor, spraying along the tiles for several yards. Well, wasn't that just *great*. I scrambled after the books, tripping over one and colliding with a seventh-grader.

"Hey, watch where you're going!" He pushed me away like I was the one in the wrong hall, instead of him.

I scowled at him. "No, *thanks*, I've got it." I bent over and picked up the first book as he and a dozen other students passed by without so much as an offer of help. Somebody kicked one of the books against a wall.

Somewhere in the middle of gathering the books, I managed to rub the eyelash away. I made it to the door of Mrs. Perez's homeroom just as the bell rang.

Through the roar of books and bodies slamming against desks, two words—separated by a pause—reached my ears as I entered the room.

"Bird. Face." A whisper, but the voice rang deep. He stood against the wall just inside the door.

The hair on the back of my neck stood up. With animal instinct, I turned only my eyes toward the sound. Time slowed while I walked past him, so close the breath from his sneering mouth rustled my hair.

Bird Face. Those two simple little words came from John Wilson, the tallest boy in eighth grade. A Brainiac, he reminded me of Frankenstein's monster. Not that he was hideous or scarred or anything. Other than his block-shaped head, he looked about as ordinary as any boy could—brown hair, brown eyes, glasses. He had bony arms and wimpy shoulders. Nothing scary about that.

But he had a way of creeping up on a person. I could be

in the library or the bus line, and all of a sudden, there he'd be, looming in my personal space. He acted like the monster in some old black-and-white movie. I had gotten somewhat used to that, but it was weird he decided to speak. And what the heck was a "bird face," anyway?

I kept walking. If John-Monster expected some kind of reaction from me, he wasn't going to get one.

I didn't stop until I got to my desk. That's when I noticed a swatch of yellow on the seat. Another sticky-note message. Still printed, but this time signed too.

Only words.

"A FREND"

And a bad speller, apparently. I examined the little square of paper for a few seconds. The writing still didn't seem familiar at all. An eerie sensation like someone was watching me made me turn. But when I glanced around the room, I got nothing.

A yellow note pad would be a clue, if only I could find one. Tookie wore a yellow shirt —designer, of course. Gayle wrote in a yellow notebook. Frank grinned at me with yellow teeth. But no yellow sticky notes anywhere in sight.

I slipped this one into my purse. At least *someone* was paying attention.

Three

I'd never be what you'd call hot.

I didn't need that boy on the bus, or John-Monster, or anyone else to tell me I'd never be hot. I knew it. Only, it never mattered before.

Notes on brutal self-assessment of appearance:

Body: Mostly straight and lean; legs with hardly any calves; waist only slightly smaller than hips; chest—without a double-A cup bra, barely any noticeable bumps under the shirt.

Sigh.

Hair: Brown—at least more the color of a Hershey bar than a mouse; long—some style possibilities, but a tendency to frizz.

Wrote "anti-frizz treatment" on my shopping list.

Complexion: Oily skin, prone to blackheads and pimples.

Added "acne medication."

Eyes: Not bad—light brown with green flecks.

"Eye shadow to enhance eye colors."

Mouth: Naturally white, straight teeth (thankfully); thin lips that almost disappear unless I smile (rarely happens).

"Plumping lip gloss."

Done.

I put the list in my purse, then dug through my underwear drawer and pulled out some money. What else could I do but work with what I had? I dressed for a bike ride to the drugstore two blocks away. A mini-makeover would start as soon as I returned.

Hair treated with anti-frizz cream and smoothed by a hot iron fell to my shoulders. Some purple eye shadow to enhance the green flecks in my eyes, my bra stuffed with cotton balls to fill out the top of my newest dress, and a cute pair of flats took me to the edge of mildly attractive. I pushed almost a week's worth of thoughts about John-Monster, the boy on the bus, and Jennifer's makeover to the back of my mind by the time Dad arrived to pick me up for lunch Sunday.

I opened the door.

"Hi, Wendy. Are you hungry?" Frowning, Dad leaned in through the doorway and studied my purple eyelids as though I'd been in a fight. "I'm going to grill us some burgers."

I wanted to scream. *Look at me, Dad, I'm almost a woman. Not a beauty, I know. But even if you had to lie, couldn't you tell me just once that I was pretty?* Like Jennifer's father told her—*all* the time. It's okay for a parent to lie about something like that, right?

Dad stepped inside.

Mom stood a few feet away, arms at her sides, forearms covered with braces.

Dad's eyes were cold as ice between the high cheekbones of his leathery Cajun face. "Hello, Cathy." His greeting sounded more like one spoken to a stranger than to someone he supposedly loved once upon a time.

Why did he have to be so cruel? Couldn't he ask how she was doing? I went over and stood next to Mom with my arms folded across my chest and glared at him.

"Hi, Pete." Mom's words caressed the air. She scanned his face as if searching for someone she used to know, then parted her lips slightly and inhaled.

"Let's go, Wendy." Dad's jaw tensed and locked.

What was his problem? I jerked my backpack off the floor and scowled at him.

"Have a good day, sweetie." Mom turned toward me. "I'll see you this evening."

"Bye. I love you." I kissed her on a cheek that was flushed and warm. *Please, Mom, don't cry.*

Dad turned, and I followed his faded blue work shirt out the door and toward his pickup truck.

Don't look back, Wendy, don't look back. If I did, Mom might run after us like she had in the beginning and grab Dad's arm as if trying to hold on to her family. I hated the way he peeled her fingers off his skin like a dirty old Band-Aid.

I didn't know who held out the longest—Mom or me—

hoping we'd be a family again. "Now we're a family of two," Mom said on the day the divorce was final, squeezing me close. Were we? It seemed that day like she'd finally given up on there being the three of us. But the way she still looked at Dad left me in doubt.

It must have been hard for her, but Mom made certain I spent Sunday afternoons and half the holidays with him. "You need to know each other as you grow up." But Dad didn't try hard enough to know the real me.

One weekend after he married my stepmother, Margaret, Dad had a surprise for my little stepbrothers and me. He was taking us somewhere he thought was special—the circus. I cried because I'd heard the trainers didn't always treat the circus animals kindly. He yelled at me for making a fuss in front of his new family. I explained why I didn't want to go, but he made me go anyway. The elephants' eyes were the saddest.

"He's the only father you have," Mom would say whenever I complained about him. "Try a little harder to get along so you won't have any regrets if something should happen to him."

Like if he died? Mom and I would be better off.

I stared out the window in silence for the entire thirty-minute ride to Dad's house and turned that idea around, considering all sides of it like a Rubik's Cube.

My stepbrother Michael was nine, and Christopher was seven and a half. I didn't want to like them, but I did.

"Wendy's here!" Christopher ran to meet me at the door.

He threw his arms around me with a force that knocked me backward. "Let's play some cards." He took me by the hand and led me to his room.

I killed some time playing with my stepbrothers while Dad grilled the burgers. When lunch was ready, each of us fixed a plate for ourselves. But instead of sitting together in the kitchen like we usually did, the boys wanted to eat outside and Dad wanted to eat at his computer. I wanted to watch a movie, so I took my plate into the family room.

"You're not allowed to eat in here." Margaret's mouth pinched into a smaller version of itself.

My cheeks stung as though I'd been slapped. I swallowed hard, forcing down the huge bite of burger I was chewing. What was the big deal?

"I always eat while I watch TV at home." My voice was as nice as I could manage with my cheeks still burning. "I'm very neat and careful not to spill anything."

Fail!

Margaret pressed her lips together in a thin line, cut me with her eyes, and walked out of the room. She went straight to Dad.

A minute later Dad stormed into the family room, his eyes bulging in their sockets and his entire head red-hot and ready to explode. "You have to follow Margaret's rules—*all* of them— just like Michael and Christopher."

It didn't matter that they ate like pigs.

Margaret stood beside Dad, a smug expression on her face.

I clenched my teeth and balled my hands into fists. *Punch her.*

"Well?" Dad glared at me.

I took a deep breath and blew it out through my mouth. "Yes, sir." *I hate you.*

Another Sunday afternoon without any smiles. What a waste of fifteen dollars and a nice outfit.

Four

"No, no, no!" I slapped the bathroom counter three times with both palms, squeezed my eyes shut, and opened them again. The stress of the previous day had left its mark, and it greeted me in the mirror. A troop of little red pimples tracked across my forehead. "Great." I heaved an exaggerated sigh. "Just what I need."

I washed my face extra, *extra* carefully, applied some acne lotion directly on the spots, and combed my bangs straight down to camouflage them. A little mascara might focus attention on my eyes.

After getting dressed, I shrugged on my backpack and grabbed hold of the straight skirt I wore, which refused to cling to my equally straight hips. I sucked in my stomach and, with both fists, gave the skirt a sharp twist to put the zipper back in its proper place on the side.

"Bye, Mom—I'm running late!" I shouted and dashed through the front door.

Mom's green Toyota was parked on the driveway, unable to be housed in the garage because of her abandoned fix-it-up projects. It sat exposed to the seesaw Louisiana weather, which only made the paint peel that much faster. Instead of the car, the garage protected heaps of junk salvaged from the neighbors' trash piles. That made a lot of sense.

Couldn't she let me back the car up and turn it around to face the street? At least that way the license plate wouldn't show. Somebody at the DMV (ha-ha-aren't-we-so-clever-and-funny) assigned the letters "HIX" to the beginning of Mom's license plate number. Mom's strong Tennessee accent didn't help the joke to be any less hilarious to people who met her and saw the plate.

For me to have a doctor or dentist appointment meant she would have to either drop me off at school or pick me up. I always asked her to use the side street. I would have stood on my head and sung "The Star-Spangled Banner" to keep Tookie and her friends from seeing that car.

I race-walked down the street and toward the bus stop, halfway between my house and Jennifer's. As usual, Mrs. Villaturo stood outside watering her flowerbed with a spray hose. Mrs. V had baked lasagna for us and brought it over right after Mom's surgery. She did that kind of thing a lot—chocolate fudge at Christmas and sugar cookies with purple, gold, and green icing at Mardi Gras. If I had a grandmother still living, she would be like Mrs. V.

"Good morning, Wendy." She brushed a strand of gray hair out of her eyes with the back of her free hand. "If you have time this afternoon, why don't you stop by for some cake? I have some new pictures of Sarah and Sam playing in the snow. It's still cold way up there in Alaska right now."

"Thanks, Mrs. V." I kept walking. "I'll try."

Next was Mr. Brown, who had just gotten off the night shift at the newspaper. He rubbed his eyes and smiled at me from behind his twin boys' stroller. The two babies bounced in their seats while a butterfly made a lazy pass in front of them.

Mr. and Mrs. Nguyen each gave me a polite nod as they loaded their four kids into their new van. They would drop the kids off at the elementary school on the way to their dry-cleaning business.

Miss Taylor's high heels tapped a cheerful beat as she walked to her mailbox carrying a short stack of envelopes. Nice business suit. If Miss Taylor could start out poor in a family of seven children and still become successful, then maybe there was hope for me.

"Wow, you're fast," she called out. "Have you ever thought about running?"

"Actually, I'm going to try out for the high school track team this week." I shouted to keep from stopping. "Tryouts start today."

"Well, good luck."

"Thanks! See you later."

I sped up my race-walk until I must have resembled a character in a silent movie, but Jennifer beat me to the bus stop. And—rats! I forgot to time myself.

"You look good with your bangs like that." If Jennifer noticed something she liked, she paid the person a compliment, stranger or not.

"Really?"

"Of course." She turned back toward the girl she had been talking to before. "Tell me about..."

I grinned and shook my head. That was Jennifer. She was friendly with everybody, but I didn't get jealous. She had chosen me as her one-and-only best friend. I remembered the day she and I met like it was yesterday.

I hadn't attended kindergarten with any of the other kids in my first-grade class, so I didn't know anyone on the first day at my new school. I stood with my face pressed against the chain-link fence and gripped it with little claw hands, thinking of home. "Don't you want to play with the other children?" the teacher on duty asked. I shook my head, and she walked away. I figured I'd better do something fast so she wouldn't come back. I was amusing myself by hanging upside-down from my knees on the monkey bars when the best upside-down smile I' d ever seen appeared before me. The person it belonged to immediately hung upside-down right next to me and started talking.

She talked for years.

"What did you do at your dad's yesterday?" Jennifer asked after we boarded the bus.

I stared blankly into space. Dad's and Margaret's unsmiling faces popped into my mind, contrasted by the faces of Jennifer's parents. I replied in a monotone, "Nothing worth talking about."

Jennifer ran her hand up and down in front of my eyes. "Well, you're still coming over after school to help me with Chanceaux and the puppies, huh?"

"Sure." I blinked before turning toward her. "I'll just have to do a few things for my mom first."

"Good."

Then she switched to the subject of her beauty makeover for the rest of the way to Bellingrath. I'd be glad when this makeover thing was history.

John-Monster skulked toward me in the cafeteria line, eyes fixed on mine, carrying his lunch tray. What did he have in mind? If I knocked the tray out of his hands first, I'd be the one in trouble.

I darted between two football players. They swayed their bulk from side to side as they lumbered through the line, and I narrowly escaped becoming the meat in a brawny sandwich. I glanced back at them. No way could those guys be only thirteen, but I was grateful for their size. John-Monster made a detour. No surprise. A Brainiac never tangled with a Jock if he could help it.

I re-entered the line, got my meal of gravel and mush, and scanned the cafeteria for a place to sit. I passed the table where Tookie and the Sticks surrounded David Griffin, who struggled to get his food down while answering their barrage of questions.

Tookie's lunch tray sat untouched. Her elbows rested on the table, hands forming a platter to prop her chin on, and she smiled at David with hot-pink lips.

I found a good spot for two as far away from John-Monster and the other Brainiacs as possible. While his friends chattered on about equations or formulas or whatever they liked to talk about, John-Monster sat on the edge of the group and stared at his plate, barely bothering with his food. Gayle Freeman watched him with sad eyes.

One of Jennifer's teachers stopped to talk to her, but she made it to our table a couple of minutes behind me.

"What's that stuck to the bottom of your milk?" She plopped down next to me.

Another note! When did that get there?

"Oh, just a piece of paper." I peeled off the yellow square and pretended to crumple it up and throw it under the table. Instead, I stuffed it into my purse.

A scientist somewhere had determined that the best time for math class was right after lunch because a full stomach supposedly made for clearer thinking on the left side of the brain. It was also the best time to nap, and if it hadn't been for Jennifer's enthusiasm for math, I would have dozed off every single day.

According to Jennifer, math was perfect because there was nothing to discuss. When she worked a math problem, the answer was either right or wrong. When it was right, that was the end of the problem. And she worked fast. Whenever possible, she asked me to time her on the day's assignment.

"Twelve minutes," I said, when she finished her worksheet. "You broke your previous record."

"Woo-hoo!" Jennifer spiked her pencil to the floor, then jumped up and did a little victory dance right in the middle of the classroom. All eyes turned her way, and Miss Carter yelled for her to sit down. We put our hands over our mouths and swallowed our laughter.

Next up was English class. I loved English! Jennifer may have liked math because it never changed, but I enjoyed the endless possibilities of language.

"The basic rules of English are immutable," Mr. Stanley once said, "but don't become so when you write."

I looked up "immutable" in the dictionary and smiled. I could be as creative as I liked in Mr. Stanley's classroom.

"Good job, Wendy." Mr. Stanley handed the previous day's assignment back to me—my composition on prunes. I had written how much I liked them and how beautiful they were. Their flavor, their color, shape, and wrinkles.

"A whole page about prunes. Can you believe it?" Tookie let out a laugh, followed by a snort. The Sticks around her looked at one another as if trying to decide whether to laugh or not. I guessed at what they were thinking: Tookie might think they were laughing at *her*.

"The assignment was an essay on the food of your choice, Miss Miller." Mr. Stanley barked at her like a bulldog with glasses, one eye squinting almost shut. He wore a multi-colored, striped button-down shirt in the kind of color combination that's left over after the year-end clearance sales: purple, pink, and orange. With it he wore a polka-dot bow tie. Some of the kids made fun of his clothes behind his back. He caught them sometimes but didn't seem to care.

On most of our literature appreciation days, Mr. Stanley took out the cello he kept in a corner of the classroom. Its tattered leather case had torn spots that looked like two eyes and a mouth—an obese little dwarf with a tall hat who watched our every move. Mr. Stanley stroked his bow feather-like across the strings of the cello. We zoned into our copies of *To Kill a Mockingbird* as he played.

"You're in charge, Wendy." Mr. Stanley's voice jerked me out of the story, leaving Scout and her problems behind.

I blinked and was back in English class. Mr. Stanley stood at the door, open just a crack, his hand on the knob. Mrs. Perez waited on the other side.

"I'll be back in a minute." Mr. Stanley said, and he followed Mrs. Perez into the hall.

I sighed. I really just wanted to read, but at least the other students wouldn't dare do anything terrible while he stood outside the door. The only thing I had to do was answer questions from poor Tammy Torino. Tammy made a good case for not funneling all eighth-graders into the same classroom.

"What do these letters mean? IV, V, VI, VII, VIII..." She held a sheet of paper Mr. Stanley had placed on everyone's desk.

"Those are Roman numerals," I said.

Her expression was blank.

"They stand for regular numbers: four, five, six, seven. You know?" I waited for a light to come on in her head, her face to show some sign of recognition.

Two ridges formed between Tammy's eyebrows. She obviously had no idea what I was talking about.

I was losing patience but did a fair job of not showing it. "That is an outline of the book you are reading. The letters stand for points in the outline." I pronounced each word slowly and distinctly.

Laughter erupted from the back of the classroom. Tookie and another Stick, Melissa, started asking idiotic questions.

"Wendy, um, can you show me how to hold my book?" Tookie held her copy of the novel in the air, upside down.

Melissa giggled.

My face grew warm. Stupid Sticks.

Jennifer stood up, scraping the legs of her desk against the floor. "Okay, no more questions." She glowered at the Sticks, and they shut up.

Jennifer turned toward me and grinned. She'd paid me back for timing her work in math class.

True friendship must have give-and-take like that.

Five

The final bell rang.

I rushed to the first-floor girls' restroom to dress for track tryouts. No way was I going to get practically naked in the gym locker room in front of a bunch of strangers. It took all year just to get used to dressing in front of the girls in my P.E. class.

Inside a stall, I took my skirt off and hung it on the door hook. I started unbuttoning my shirt when an awful sound came from the next stall over. Someone was throwing up. Nice. Maybe it was an epidemic, it was happening often enough.

"Are you all right?" If I got my clothes on fast, I could give her a wet paper towel.

A whimper came first, followed by a flush and the door unlatching. It swung open wide and banged against the front of my stall. Through the crack, I caught a glimpse of red hair and a girl darting from the restroom.

Oh, well. Give me credit for trying.

I left the stall wearing a t-shirt, shorts, and Reeboks. I dropped my backpack to the floor and stood on my toes to stretch my calves, repeating the up and down motion to pump them up as far as they would go. Why did my legs have to be so skinny? Well, at least they were somewhat tan now.

I picked up the backpack and slung it over my shoulder. What was that stuck to the edge of the sink—right across from where I'd changed? A yellow sticky-note. A chill went up my spine. This was getting creepy, especially if a boy was writing the notes. Who else had been in the restroom besides the sick girl?

With slow, quiet steps I approached the note, looking behind me and keeping my ears open for the slightest sound, in case the person was still there.

Good luck.

A FREND

That was sweet, I guessed, in a Boo Radley sort of way. If there was such a thing as a kind-hearted stalker. It was freaky that this person knew my every move. And why not just wish me luck to my face? I had no time to figure anything out right then, or I'd be late for tryouts. I dropped the note into my backpack, stepped one foot into the hall, then gasped and jerked back.

John-Monster walked toward me in the same direction as the athletic field where I needed to go.

My stomach flipped.

Okay, Wendy, don't give him the satisfaction of changing

course. Start walking and keep walking. Head high. I set my jaw and focused my eyes on a tree in the far distance, then made my way toward my destination.

Long-legged John-Monster quickly gained on me. Something like static electricity bounced off my skin, as if my body was trying to repel him. The hair on my arms stood up. My senses heightened. I was aware of the breath rushing from his nostrils, his clicking jaw, the musty odor of his clothes. This must have been how the rabbit felt that Angel once cornered in the backyard before we rescued it.

"Oh-hhh…Bird Face has bird legs." He whined with fake pity.

I held my breath until he passed, waited until I thought he couldn't see my face, then squeezed my eyes shut and stretched my mouth wide in a silent scream. I finally opened my eyes and caught my reflection next to his in the glass wall ahead.

He was laughing.

Track coaches and muscular student helpers from the mega-sized public high school herded us eighth-graders to designated spots on the field.

"You! Little bit! Yeah, you. Come over here." A beefy index finger beckoned.

I trudged over and joined a group of girls waiting in line to do the long jump. *Rats.* All I really wanted to do for track was run. Running gave me that feeling of escape from everything I hated about my life, leaving it all behind, even for a little while.

Jumping would only get me a few feet away—or a few yards at best. I needed to run.

Gayle stood first in line. She took off her glasses and handed them to a high school girl with gladiator legs who held a clipboard.

"Go!"

Gayle took off running and leapt into the air, kicking as if struggling against an unseen predator. She landed on the sand beyond. *Whump.* A high school boy ran over and measured the distance. Two coaches standing together with arms crossed and feet spread apart spoke to each other in low voices.

Was it good? Was it bad?

Gladiator Legs returned Gayle's glasses. The process repeated itself for each girl in front of me.

My turn came. I focused. I ran. I started my jump.

"Bird Face!"

My concentration disintegrated, along with my flow of motion. The jump ended short, and I landed on my butt. Hard.

Aaghh! With so little padding, my tailbone took a direct hit. Stars burst like fireworks in front of my eyes. I pressed my hand against my backside and rocked in pain. John-Monster laughed and pointed. Everyone on our end of the field turned toward me and stared.

Just let me sink into the dirt and die.

"You all right?" Beefy Index Finger grabbed me by both arms and yanked me to my feet before I could answer.

I'd had enough agony for one day. I grabbed my stuff and

left the tryouts without getting to show anybody how fast I could run. I ran all the way home.

Six

That evening, I told Mom about the name-calling and asked what she thought about it. I could count on her to tell me the truth.

She brushed my arm with her fingers as she offered an explanation. "He's saying you have a big nose, honey."

I opened my eyes so wide my eyelids stretched. "What?"

"I'm sorry, but that's what 'bird face' means." Her voice was tender, but her words stung just the same.

My hands flew to the sides of my nose. "He has a bigger nose than *mine*!"

"In that case, he has a lot of nerve, but that's what he's talking about."

"But I can't do anything about that." It sounded like a whine, but at least I wasn't like Eddie Andrew, who chose not to shower or use deodorant and got teased about his smell.

"I know it's a mean thing to do." She crinkled her eyes and pressed her lips together.

I sighed. If somebody had offered me a million dollars right then and there, it wouldn't have mattered. The sneer on John-Monster's face made sense now. He thought I was ugly. And if *he* did, who else?

I walked to the dresser and picked up a hand mirror to get a really close view. My face was skinny like my body. My jaw and chin were small, and my long, pointy nose stuck out pretty far beyond them.

Arrrrr! I hated John-Monster, but I hated myself even more for caring what he thought. I slammed the little mirror onto the top of the dresser.

"Try not to let this upset you too much." Mom joined me in front of the dresser. With a brace-covered arm, she tucked my hair behind one ear. "You just have an unusual-looking face, that's all. One I love."

My shoulders slumped. "You're not helping, Mom."

"You wouldn't want to look like anyone but yourself, would you?" She tilted her head and smiled. "Besides, no one knows what they'll look like when they grow up, anyway. Everyone changes."

"I sure hope so." I studied her pretty face and recalled Dad's strong jaw line and full mouth. Who did I look like? Maybe I was adopted.

"You know, somebody in John's life may be making fun of him in some way. Rejection makes people do things they wouldn't ordinarily do." She kissed the top of my head and walked out, closing the door behind her.

Good. I hoped somebody *was* making fun of him. I'd have to remind myself of that every time John-Monster headed my direction. Still, I'd try to avoid him like the cockroach he was.

Before going to bed, I sat at the computer and searched the Internet for "bird face." Results: a fashion designer, a rock band, and a deformity.

A deformity? There it was, including photos, on the same website as Bernard Bellingrath's tail (another person's tail, not his tail—at least I don't think it was his).

Bird face: the common name for a medical abnormality in which the nose is large and beak-like and the jaw is small or not in a forward position as it should be.

A worm of misery twisted in my gut. Horrible faces screamed at me from the photographs. I wasn't deformed, really, but I did see a little of myself in them. I wasn't normal, that's for sure. And no makeup, no hairstyle would fix this face. I was doomed to start high school as a freak. Heaven help me if John-Monster followed me to the same school. The torment would never end.

I shrieked and threw myself on the bed, grabbed a pillow and punched it. If only it was John-Monster's face! Then I had an idea and sat up. What if I paid the bus driver to run him over? *Forgive me, God; that's horrible.* But what if the bus got close enough to scare the pants off him? I'd have a camera to capture the expression on his stupid face, and I'd laugh at him through the bus window. If I did something like that every time he called me Bird Face...

But I was being ridiculous. I didn't have enough money for a camera or the bus driver. My heart sank. Was that how Barney felt—hopeless?

Sweet little Barney, growing up with a tail. The teasing. His innocent face. Junior high—terrible. *Poor thing!*

Funny how you can live your days as a clueless little kid, believing you look just fine—with a crooked tooth or knobby knees or *a bird face*—until someone, usually someone you don't even care about, knocks you in the heart with it.

Seven

And then there was David Griffin, who never said a mean thing to anyone.

David. We had homeroom and Louisiana history class together in the mornings and attended the same church on Sundays. Adorable. Curly brown hair, green eyes to die for, played baseball. Cute enough to have been a Suave, but too self-confident for a clique. He was the only boy I didn't mind going to school with.

"Hi, Wendy."

My heart beat like the drums for kick-off at the start of football season. "Hey," I said, as we entered homeroom at the same time.

David's face lit up. "I thought I saw you running past the track field yesterday." He passed his desk and continued to walk with me to mine, spoiling an attack by John-Monster, who waited for me again inside the door.

"Yeah, that was me." *Oh, no—did he see me at the long jump?* I grinned, but my mouth was so dry that my lip stuck to my teeth on one side, like a snarl.

"You sure can run."

I ran my tongue over my teeth to unstick the lip, then swallowed. "Thanks." And my mind went blank. Like a ventriloquist's dummy, my mouth opened and slammed shut again. *Say something—fast—or he'll think you're stuck up.* Nothing. Not even about a TV show from last night, because there wasn't time to watch much anymore. I waited. *Come on, David. Ask me a question so I can answer it.*

He didn't, so I didn't. I went straight to my desk and sat down. Idiot.

Did I hurt his feelings? Maybe David was supposed to be someone important in my life. And I'd already missed a lot of chances to talk to him. I really messed this up.

In my peripheral vision, I followed him. He took his seat two rows over.

Tookie, who sat in the row between us, extended her long, tan-in-a-bottle legs into the aisle closest to David, toes pointed in his direction. "Hi, David." She smiled with hot-pink lips and flipped her neon red hair over her shoulder.

Uh-oh. My ship was sinking, David was overboard, and Tookie had the lifeboat. David had taken Tookie to the Spring Dance. *She* had asked *him*, but still, he didn't put up much of a fight, rumor had it. Underneath all that makeup and fake tan, she was still better looking than most of the other girls in eighth grade. Especially me.

What chance did a Bird Face with bird legs have against somebody like that? If I were good-looking, maybe it wouldn't matter that my personality stank. Really, Tookie didn't have a good personality either. She just knew how to use what nature had given her—and to flirt. Or give fake compliments to somebody to get what she wanted. Boys always fell for it. And some girls did too.

I'd been shortchanged. I slouched down in my chair and sulked, then sneaked a peek at Tookie chattering away at David. You'd have thought she actually knew something about baseball, the way she went on and on about it. What was so great about making small talk anyway? It was useless. Until I met David, that is.

When people would ask me, "How are you?" they really didn't want to know. They probably expected me to say "Fine," which was a stupid answer—especially if I wasn't fine at the time—so I always replied with a loud, enthusiastic "Great!" instead. Then they'd jerk back in surprise, as if they'd tried to pick up a moth they thought was dead, but wasn't.

Now, if someone asked me a *real* question, that was another story. I'd talk awhile, then say something that sounded rude without meaning to. I couldn't count the number of times I'd ended a conversation that way. Some people might think, *So what—they'll get over it.* But they didn't live in my world.

And then there was Alice—quiet, overweight, and pink. Pink

hair, pink skin, pink teeth, and so many pimples they made her face super-pink. No mother, according to Tookie, so that's why she didn't know how to get rid of the pimples. Maybe I should tell her about my acne lotion.

After homeroom, a Suave cornered Alice in the hall. "Pizza face!" Some airheaded girls walking with him giggled.

Alice's eyes filled with hurt. She rushed to the restroom, her clarinet case rattling against her side. *Should I follow her?* I didn't. Instead, I let her suffer alone. What was wrong with me?

Later, when I passed by my locker, a folded yellow sticky-note protruded from the crack.

Speak up.

A FREND

Eight

Louisiana History class. I walked along the folding tables; the three-dimensionals were awesome. Early Native Louisianians. The First European Settlement. The Louisiana Purchase. About half the class had turned theirs in already, including me.

I pretended to study what I saw but kept an eye on David as we moved around the displays. He said something nice about each and every project and asked a few questions too. I could listen to him talk all day.

I stopped in front of a panorama of The Battle of New Orleans. "That would look better if it was turned the other way." Trying to be helpful, I pointed at—well, it really didn't matter what.

Silence. Everyone's eyes turned directly on *me*. Including David's.

"Not cool, Wendy," Tookie said. She stroked David's hand and fluttered her eyelashes.

Just my luck. The name printed on the base of the project: David Griffin.

Way to go, Wendy.

Curiosity about who made the track team was eating me alive. I counted the minutes waiting to get out of science class and into the hall again.

"Here are your pop quizzes from last Friday." Mr. Guzman frowned and shook his head.

Ugh. Bad news. I rubbed the back of my neck.

Mr. Guzman handed a stack of papers to the first person in each row of desks. The papers moved down the assigned rows. When they got to me, I flipped through for mine. Where was it? I searched again. Nothing.

Before I could raise my hand, someone behind me snickered. John-Monster held his test paper in the air and mouthed the letter "A." Then he held mine up and mouthed the letter "C" while rubbing an imaginary tear from his eye.

I whipped back around. This was one of those cockroach moments, when you fear you may have to get close enough to the pest to get rid of it. Just in time, Mr. Guzman snatched my paper from John-Monster and handed it to me.

I cut my eyes toward him. Geez, it was only a pop quiz. What a competitive sicko.

"Bird Face," he mouthed.

I sauntered down the first-floor hallway, and glanced at posters and displays along the way. Like I was killing time or waiting to go home. The bulletin board with the track team list was just ahead. I paused in front of a gigantic sports awards case and pretended to study the trophies and photographs of Bellingrath athletes.

John-Monster's older brother Jeff was there. He'd played on every single school team there was when I was in sixth grade and he was in eighth. Photographs of him in baseball, basketball, and football uniforms—trophies in hand—filled one whole shelf. His smiling father stood next to him in a picture, a hand on Jeff's shoulder.

Mr. Wilson was one of the biggest supporters of Bellingrath's athletic programs, not to mention president of the Booster Club three years running. Funny thing, though. The Wilson Jock Gene had sidestepped John-Monster. He wasn't on any of the teams.

Boom—a burst of air from the administration office door. I turned.

Speak of the devil.

Mr. Wilson, his hand clamped on John-Monster's shoulder, stormed out of the office. John-Monster hung his head. Mr. Wilson scowled and shoved him into the hall.

I snickered. Nice to see John-Monster on the receiving end for a change.

After the hallway cleared, I approached the bulletin board. I searched the list of those who'd made the cut, for one name and one name only: John Wilson. It wasn't there.

My heart warmed. No need to hire the bus driver after all.

Nine

Jennifer held onto the barre on her bedroom's mirrored wall. She swung her right leg out behind her, then forward and up, moving with the same kind of precision she used to solve math problems. Her black leotard stretched with her like a second skin. She rested the heel of her arched foot on the barre and bent over the leg until her chin touched it.

I'd tried that—once. *Ouch.* I clenched my teeth.

Jennifer raised her torso, caught my expression in the mirror, and laughed. "Cut it out. You've seen me do this, like a thousand times." Her hair was pulled back into the tighter-than-tight bun required by Madame Smith for intermediate and advanced students.

Jennifer had studied ballet as long as I'd known her, and I'd never missed one of her recitals until it happened to take place on the same day as Mom's surgery. I was probably more disappointed about it than she was.

"My costume is back from the cleaners." She lowered her leg to the floor, took one step and performed a pirouette, then a grand jete leap to her closet. She opened the door and pulled out a shoebox and a plastic bag containing a dress of white cotton candy.

I helped her place them on the bed.

"Look at the pointe shoes." Her eyes sparkled as she opened the box full of satin and ribbons.

"Awesome, Jen." I ran a finger along one of the ribbons.

"Want to try them on? We wear the same shoe size."

"Sure!" I reached in with both hands and lifted them out.

Jennifer handed me a pair of toe covers. I slipped on the shoes, and Jennifer helped me wrap the ribbons around my ankles.

I wobbled on my toes a bit, then arched my feet as far as they would go so I could maintain my balance. A little pain, but worth it.

"Wow, your legs and feet are strong for somebody who doesn't dance." Jennifer surveyed the length of my legs. "Good shape to your calves."

I studied my image in the wall mirror. Hey, the legs didn't look so scrawny. The calves did show more definition than a few weeks before. All that bike peddling to Jennifer's to take care of the puppies, no doubt.

John-Monster's insult about my legs on the day of track tryouts surfaced in my mind. "They don't look like bird legs?" I tilted my head and scrunched my nose.

"No, silly."

I smiled at Jennifer and sat down on a chair to unlace the shoes. There was a time when I longed to take ballet with her, to be one of those twirling little princesses on the stage, decked out in sequins and tulle. But Mom couldn't afford the lessons or the costumes, and she refused to ask Dad for help. After a few weeks of feeling sorry for myself, I got over it.

Now I focused on my own talent. I could draw—just about anything or anybody—even before taking an art class in school. It was one of the things about me that Jennifer appreciated, and she put my artistic ability to good use every chance she got.

"I'm sick of all this pink." She spread her arms wide and twisted at the waist to take in the entire room. "You know what I'm thinking about doing?"

"What?"

She grinned. "Black and white." She clenched her fists and bounced on her toes. "It's so in!"

That was my invitation. "Give me something to sketch on."

Whether she had an idea for redecorating her room or designing a poster for school, she came to me to put it on paper.

"Look at the idea Wendy had for my room. Isn't it cool?" She practically knocked her mother down in the hallway and shoved my sketch in her face.

I didn't mind taking the blame for a complete re-do of Jennifer's room. Mrs. Sampson probably knew better than to believe that anyway.

Cynthia T. Toney

A good thing I was interested in art, 'cause what cheaper hobby could there be? A pencil or pen or felt marker was always lying around, and almost anything could be a drawing surface. The most interesting drawing papers were the ones most people didn't think of, like wrinkled brown packing paper stuffed in a box being thrown out.

Art books always topped my wish list for each birthday and Christmas. I had a nice collection of them started already, including some on faces, figure drawing, and perspective, as well as art history. My favorite artist of all time was van Gogh. On my list of things to do before I graduated from high school was "See an original van Gogh painting."

But when I was seven, I learned not everyone appreciates seeing talent in others, especially when they haven't discovered their own yet. At a kid's birthday party, I took part in a drawing contest. The lights were turned off, and we were asked to draw a birthday cake. The room was so dark I couldn't see the paper, the crayon, my hand, or anything. But in my mind's eye, I imagined a cake with burning candles on it. Working only from touch, I used my fingers to measure shapes and spaces. I pictured the crayon drawing the lines where I wanted them. And I won. The grownups said the cake looked real, right down to the candle flames. "You cheated," one of the other kids said. I stared at her like she was crazy.

After that, I began to visualize each drawing before I began it, just as Jennifer learned to visualize every dance move before she executed it. We saw our futures in the arts, so we took advantage

66

of every opportunity to use our talents at school. The really big chance came along as we neared the end of eighth grade.

Ten

The Spring Program. It should have been held in fall or winter. Instead, it was set for the end of the school year so we'd be too busy to get into trouble, waiting to be sprung from junior high prison.

It would take place right after final exams and right before we received our report cards. After cramming our brains and losing sleep, we'd use our last ounce of physical strength to sing and dance and blow wind instruments. That should break our spirits.

In spite of it all, it really was pretty cool. It always started with a concert, followed by a magician or comedy act. Then it finished with a play or musical. Families and other volunteers pitched in and donated supplies, made refreshments, and sewed costumes. All that for something held in the gym.

This year, everybody would be put to the test whipping

out a condensed version of the musical *Oklahoma*. And the way Jennifer and I had it figured, it had better be good. Our reputations depended on it.

"Wendy, how'd you like to handle the stage scenery and props?" My art teacher from last year, Mrs. Guidry, had caught me in the hall one afternoon around Mardi Gras. Charcoal streaked across part of her upper lip, like half a moustache. Red paint dotted her hair.

"Yes! Thanks, Mrs. Guidry." I walked around with a goofy grin on my face the rest of the day.

By the next day, I'd searched for *Oklahoma* on the web and started doing some designs. My heart somersaulted. This was my Big Chance—my first public art project and best opportunity to showcase my talent. I'd prove to everybody at school I had what it took to be a professional artist someday.

By the day after that, I was a wreck. This could also be my epic fail.

Jennifer had more of a sure thing. In early April, she'd auditioned for the lead role of Laurey Williams. She competed against several other girls, including none other than Tookie Miller. The way Tookie pranced around like a show horse afterward, you'd have thought she won the part already. But Jennifer's friendly personality and wholesome good looks must've impressed the judges.

On a Friday morning, the cast list was posted on the main bulletin board outside the administration office.

"I made it!" Jennifer grinned and squealed and bounced on

her toes.

"I knew you could do it." I wrapped my arms around her in a bear hug. "Congratulations, Jen." I tried to bounce with her but had to let go to avoid getting my feet crushed.

"Thanks!" She squealed again, then turned and thanked everyone around us too.

"Humph." Tookie flipped a wave of red hair back over her shoulder and shoved past us with her nose in the air. The Sticks rallied around her.

"Oh Tookie, you were so much better than her."

"That song you sang for audition was great."

"Your hair was fixed so cute, and your makeup was perfect."

Tookie's eyes clouded, and her hot-pink lips drooped. I almost felt sorry for her.

That afternoon, Mr. Stanley and the music teacher distributed scripts and music for performers to begin learning their parts over the weekend.

"Will you help me learn my lines after school?" Jennifer stuck out her bottom lip and made puppy dog eyes.

"Of course." Did she even have to ask? "Hey, let's see if Mr. Stanley will let us go to the gym and see my stage stuff."

Jennifer and I cornered Mr. Stanley at his desk. I whispered, "Please let us go so I can show Jennifer." He gave us passes.

Tookie must have heard or guessed what was going on, because she crossed her arms and pouted. As I closed the classroom door on the way out, she glared at us through the little glass pane.

When we reached the gym, a crowd of sweaty boys stampeded in through the double doors with the sign reading "NO Cleats, NO Spike Heels." They headed for the showers. Was that David coming in from baseball practice? My heart raced.

Jennifer yanked my arm. "Earth to Wendy. What are you looking at?"

"Nothing. Just around."

"You kind of like him, don't you?" The corners of her mouth curled upward slightly.

"Who?"

She snorted and shook her head. "Never mind."

What a relief. Spill my guts about David? Not even to Jennifer. I couldn't explain why not. I couldn't even explain to myself how just seeing another human being could make me so happy.

"Wow," Jennifer said when she saw my pattern for the fake surrey with the fringe on top.

I'd drawn it on a large roll of newsprint paper laid out on the gym floor. I designed the surrey so the actors could sit on stools hidden behind it and appear to drive the fake horse I planned to draw. One of the parents would cut my patterns out of plywood, assemble everything, and add supports so the surrey and horse would stand up by themselves. Then the props would be returned to me to paint.

Working on *Oklahoma* was a blast. More than that, the gym was John-Monster-free. What luck—for a while.

Eleven

The. Big. Makeover. Day.

Saturday, and I was home. Jennifer had promised she'd take care of Chanceaux and the puppies by herself before she left for her appointment.

At the sound of a car door slamming, I ran to the window and peeked through the blinds. Mrs. Sampson's black BMW backed out of the driveway at the same time the doorbell rang.

On the porch stood someone who looked sort of like Jennifer, only a whole lot older. Grinning from ear to ear and clenching her fists, she let out an excited scream.

I nearly screamed myself, but for different reasons.

Her face was covered with makeup—more than my old babysitter used to wear. I couldn't even see her freckles. Gone was the silky straight hair I would've given anything to own. Instead, she wore a complicated style with layers of loose curls held in place with spray or gel or something.

This was a nightmare. Now she looked more grown up, more sophisticated, more beautiful than ever. Could I possibly feel any uglier?

All right, I had to get hold of myself and deal with it. It wasn't Jennifer's fault I inherited some bad genes.

I took a deep breath and faked a smile. "You look fabulous!"

"Girls, come inside. It's a hot day, and the air conditioner is running." Mom spoke from the kitchen sink, her back toward us.

"Hi, Mrs. Robichaud." Jennifer walked into the kitchen like a fashion model and stopped in that crazy pose they always do at the end of the runway.

Mom turned around, and an awkward pause followed. Her face froze in an expression of shock and curiosity combined— like the face of the mouse we surprised on the night we moved in. The mouse recovered. Mom might not. Did she even recognize Jennifer?

"Jen had a makeover," I said, to help Mom out.

Her eyelids made two rapid blinks. "Oh, hello, Jen. It's good to see you." She half-smiled. I waited a sec to see if she'd comment on the makeover. She didn't.

I needed to shift the attention to something else—fast. "Jen, want to help me with an idea for the *Oklahoma* set?"

Jennifer flipped a long curl of hair away from her face. "Sorry, I can't. My dad wants to take some pictures of my mom and me while we look like this."

Must be nice to have a father who cared about stuff like that.

"Well, call me later, okay? We can go over some of your lines."

"Okay, I will." She headed out the door.

Mrs. Sampson pulled into the driveway again to pick Jennifer up. I didn't wait to hear the car door.

I had to get out of there—to avoid questions or comments from Mom and to hide the tears stinging my eyes. I escaped to the bathroom but found no comfort in staring at my reflection in the mirror. I placed my hands on the sides of my head and pulled the hair away from my face. There was no denying it: Jennifer and I didn't look like we belonged together anymore.

She was changing and leaving me behind.

I forked the red beans and rice into smaller piles on my dinner plate. Maybe Mom wouldn't notice I hadn't taken a single bite. One of my favorite dishes too. She was obviously trying to cheer me up, so I nibbled a few grains of rice and sneaked a piece of sausage into my napkin.

"May I be excused?"

"Well…sure, honey."

I ran to my room and pulled a box of old photographs from the closet. I had to figure it out—the day, the month, even the year it happened. When did my body take the nasty turn from cute little kid to unsightly teenager with a big honker?

At the top of the pile was a print labeled on the back in Mom's handwriting, "Pete with Wendy, age 6." Dad and I were flying a bright red kite against a clear blue sky in front of our old house. Something grabbed my heart and squeezed it. It was so good being with him back then. We had fun together, and I was happy. Would we ever have a day like that together again? I sighed and set the photo on my nightstand before closing the box.

The Dad I once knew. Would he make it to the Spring Program to see all the work I'd done for *Oklahoma*? Or would it be just Mom and me again, as usual? Jennifer didn't have that problem. Both of her parents, and maybe all four of her grandparents, would be there. Same with most of the other kids.

If I invited Dad, would he actually come? I shook my head. No, I'd wind up disappointed again. He'd find a reason not to make it, like dozens of times before. Or worse, he'd say he'd be there but not show. No phone call. Later I'd overhear a conversation between him and Mom that he'd done something else—*with* someone else—instead.

On the bed, I pulled my knees to my chest and stretched my t-shirt over them, hugging them tight.

An idea! I popped my legs back out again from under the t-shirt. *I know—I'll put it in writing.* Even Dad couldn't ignore a formal invitation.

I jumped to my feet and dug some stationery out of the nightstand drawer. Leaning my back against the headboard of my bed, I propped a lap desk on my knees and composed a letter. I carefully chose the words.

Dear Dad,

Although I visit you almost every Sunday, there's something I need to ask you, and I feel more comfortable asking you in writing.

The Spring Program is on the last Friday in May at 7:00 p.m. Will you please try to attend?

The main part of the program is the musical "Oklahoma" (a short version of it, so don't worry). I designed and painted most of the stage decorations for it.

The school is going to keep all the work I did, and it's too big to bring home anyway. The only way you'll get to see it is if you come to the Spring Program.

Please say you'll be there and won't let anything stop you. I won't ask for anything else all summer (not even for my birthday) if you'll come and sit with Mom and me.

Love,

Wendy

I stamped and addressed the envelope to Pete Robichaud and placed it on top of my backpack. I'd mail it in the morning.

Maybe this time would be different.

Twelve

Rehearsals for *Oklahoma* began the following Monday. I helped Jennifer on our bus rides to and from school—listening, coaching, and standing in while she practiced her lines.

In one scene, Jennifer had to act like she was pretending to be brave while really feeling vulnerable on the inside.

Me as Jud Fry: "You didn't wanna be wit' me by yerself; not a minute more'n you had to."

Jennifer as Laurey: "Why, I don't know what you're talkin' about. I'm with you here by myself now, ain't I?"

Me as Jud: "You wouldn'ta been, if you had the chance."

I totally got Laurey now, being around such a creep. It was like me with John-Monster. Too much so. I had to stop.

"Um, Jen, can you take a look at these sketches?" I stuck my sketchpad in front of her face. "The stage manager wants *so* much scenery, I'm at a loss."

She laid down the script and took the sketchpad from my hand without grumbling. "Okay." She turned the pages and studied each sketch. "You can combine that barrel with that tree and draw that wagon in front of that fence." She handed the pad back to me.

Jennifer knew that true friendship must have give-and-take like that.

Ugh. The dreaded prep for final exams. Normal class work came to a halt as teachers began their mind-numbing reviews. If a topic bored you the first time around, imagine a hundred of those a day. You wished for *death*.

The upside? Some of us in the Spring Program, like Jennifer and me, were excused from class! We got review sheets to take home and study. Not to be harsh, but teachers really needed to concentrate on people like Tammy Torino.

Of course, Jennifer and I were thrilled. Almost the entire school day to do the things we loved.

The downside? My envy grew.

With the know-how Jennifer got from her makeover session, she now wore just enough makeup to look terrific. Add that to a tamed version of her new hairstyle, and she rocked.

"You look so sophisticated, Jennifer." After lunch, Melissa broke ranks from the Sticks hanging out under the oak tree. She approached Jennifer. "Come over here with us."

Jennifer wasn't one to be told where to stand. She always went wherever she wanted, invited or not. She just never wanted to stand under the oak tree with a bunch of Sticks before. I tagged along, and nobody complained—not out loud, anyway.

The Sticks gathered around her like she was the newest color in the crayon box. Tookie crossed her arms and pressed her hot-pink lips together. She was steaming mad. Her ears turned as red as her hair.

The Suaves fell all over themselves trying to talk to Jennifer after that. But acknowledge *my* existence? Of course not.

How long would it be before people started asking who that ugly girl was with Jennifer Sampson?

My projects lined an entire wall inside the gym. Spectacular! I covered my silly grin with one hand. *Thank you, Mrs. Guidry, for getting me this gig.*

"Wendy, they look so real," Tammy said, her eyes wide with wonder.

Maybe I'd been too hard on her in English class.

"You got the proportions just right." Mrs. Guidry nodded and patted me on the back.

"Such nice detail." That from a volunteer.

My envy toward Jennifer faded, and I went to work. Once the creative right side of my brain kicked in, a peaceful bubble surrounded and isolated me from everything else. I was in my own little world until…

John-Monster, who somehow won a small non-speaking role, was let out of captivity and found the time to saunter over.

"Bird Fa-a-a-ce," he said in a long whisper, taking his time walking by.

My bubble burst and my throat squeezed shut. I racked my brain for an insult to fire back at him, but nothing.

Ignore him. I turned my back toward him and flipped through my sketchpad.

Remember, somebody probably makes fun of him too. No, that didn't make me feel better. He was just plain mean. Jerk.

He kept moving.

Good. Back to work.

I turned toward the horse I'd just finished painting.

No! A long, heavy black line, like from a wide-tipped felt marker, streaked across it.

I screamed. He'd destroyed it. Murdered it. The image of the horse pulsated before my eyes. My head throbbed. I whipped around, but he'd disappeared. And no witnesses. Or maybe nobody cared.

"I hope you die, John Wilson," I said between clenched teeth. I dropped the sketchpad and rubbed my temples.

The surrey! Hours of work—all those details! I rushed a few yards down the wall to it, then breathed a sigh of relief. It was okay. But on its wheel was a yellow sticky-note.

It's his problem.

A FREND

Thirteen

A siren screamed from the blue and white police car speeding past our buses in front of school the next morning. The car skidded to a stop so close to the steps I clenched my teeth and waited for a crash. The siren died with a pitiful moan, lights still flashing from the car's roof. A young male officer hopped out of the passenger seat and hurried inside.

"Can you see what's going on?" I asked Jennifer. She towered over me where I sat on the bus. Both of us were crushed against the window as everybody from the other side of the aisle moved over to our side.

"No, I can't see a thing, but I guess nobody blew up the science lab or anything like that. No smoke."

"I wonder if somebody's getting arrested." I'd had my eye on one of the volunteers for the Spring Program. He was too weird, staring at the girls all the time.

We continued to speculate about the cause of all the excitement. Entertaining, until some of the comments got downright cruel.

"Maybe old man Stanley finally croaked." One of the Suaves made a choking sound.

"Or somebody hit him over the head with his cello," another one said. A roar of laughter followed.

I sickened at the thought of harm coming to Mr. Stanley and scowled at the Suaves. If anybody had to be hurt or dead, let it be John-Monster instead.

When our bus got to the front of the line, Jennifer and I stumbled out and sprinted to the building. An Emergency Medical Services vehicle tore across the lawn behind us, its siren wailing. It parked alongside the police car.

Inside, we bypassed our lockers. Everybody was headed straight for Mrs. Perez's room.

"Go to your homerooms!" Mrs. Perez spread her arms and legs wide, her petite frame blocking the rear entrance of her classroom.

Miss Carter manned the front entrance, directing traffic like a cop. "Keep moving!" She motioned with her arms. "You know where you belong!"

Relief swept over me when I spotted Mr. Stanley.

"Get out of there," he barked at some boys trying to poke their heads past Mrs. Perez to get a peek inside. He clapped a burly hand on one boy's shoulder to pull him away.

"Hey, you can't touch me." The boy jerked his shoulder

loose.

Mr. Stanley confronted him. "So sue me. Now, get your butt out of here."

With a nod from Mrs. Perez, Jennifer and I slipped through the crowd and into the room.

The public address system came to life and issued a belated command: "Anyone remaining in the hall must proceed immediately to the cafeteria."

Yeah, right.

Everyone in homeroom had gathered in the center, strangely quiet, eyes focused on one spot. Through the gaps between people's legs and desks, I made out the bottoms of a pair of shoes, toes pointing up. Jennifer pushed her way through to the body, and I squeezed in behind her.

On the floor lay Tookie, flat on her back in the aisle. Why was she wearing jeans and a long-sleeved shirt buttoned over a t-shirt on such a hot day? And her face! She looked like a mummy with hollowed-out cheeks. The circles under her closed eyes were almost black against her skin and her scalp was visible through thinning red hair. Someone had clumsily rolled up a shirtsleeve, but Tookie never would have done it that way. Were they looking for needle marks? Did they find any?

Jennifer and I gaped at each other, then slammed our mouths shut.

"She fainted," David said, squatting next to Tookie. His eyes were clouded with concern.

"Back away, everybody." It was Mrs. Perez. "Give them

plenty of room."

The broad-shouldered young policeman parted the crowd. Two emergency medical technicians followed.

The female EMT opened Tookie's eyelids and examined her pupils, then searched for a pulse.

"What's your name, son?" the policeman asked David.

"David Griffin." His voice cracked.

"Thank you." Gaudin, the badge read. *God's peace.* "Let's step aside now." He spoke with kindness.

David got up and moved away from Tookie, and the male tech fastened a blood pressure cuff to her arm and pumped the bulb.

Officer Gaudin took a notepad from his pocket. "What happened?" He directed the question to David.

"She was standing here talking to me. Then her eyes rolled back and she fell against her desk, and her head hit the floor."

Officer Gaudin scribbled something down.

The female tech unbuttoned Tookie's shirt, stuck a stethoscope to her chest, and listened.

"Are you the teacher?" Gaudin asked Mrs. Perez.

"Yes, I am."

"What do you know about this girl?"

Mrs. Perez lowered her voice. "She's anorexic."

We were standing close enough to hear, and we gasped. Others must have heard too because shouts and whispers broke out all over the room. "Oh, no!" "Poor Tookie." "No way!"

"She's crazy," John-Monster blurted.

Gaudin turned sharply toward John-Monster and cleared his throat. He extended an arm and led Mrs. Perez away from the crowd.

She swallowed and took a deep breath before speaking in a whisper again—only not low enough. "Her parents have been getting psychiatric help for her."

I stared at Tookie lying on the floor like a flower deprived of water. Once proud and beautiful, now tossed to the ground and wilted.

"I thought it was helping," Mrs. Perez continued, the words barely audible through fingers she held against her lips.

The female tech moved the stethoscope from one place to another across Tookie's abdomen. Her ribcage could have been from the skeleton in science class, with skin stretched over it. I had to look away, or I'd faint and wind up on the floor myself.

Skin and bones, Mrs. V would have said.

Fourteen

Mrs. Sampson sat stone-faced behind the wheel of her car as it crept through the St. Luke's Hospital parking garage. Jennifer wanted me with her. And then my mom wanted to come along, so there we all were.

None of us spoke as the car worked its way higher and higher, passing row after row of vehicles. A moonless night made the drive through the gray concrete enclosure about as sad and miserable as it could get. I shifted positions in my seat. Jennifer leaned her head against the door and stared out the window. Reaching the top but finding nothing, Mrs. Sampson began a slow descent. When I'd almost given up and thought we'd have to park on the street, a place opened up near the bottom where we started.

In the hospital, a young woman with a phony-looking smile greeted us at the information desk. "May I help you?"

"We're here to see a girl named Tookie Miller," Mrs. Sampson said, but didn't return the smile.

We took the elevator, and I worked to keep my dinner down. Was it the lurching starts and stops or something else? We traveled to the fourth floor, and the elevator doors opened to a waiting area. Lit up like a sunny day, it still managed to be depressing. Drab and colorless, except for the people there.

A man with a tanned face, slick graying hair, and a dark suit paced the shiny white tiles behind a row of chairs. A slim red-haired woman, fashion-magazine perfect, sat upright in one of the chairs. Could that be Tookie's mother? She held a handkerchief and rubbed her folded arms. A red-haired boy about eight years old sat next to her, his eyes closed, chin touching his chest.

"Ann," Mrs. Sampson said to the woman.

The man stopped pacing and stared at us. His eyes were bloodshot and his jaw clenched tight.

"Oh, Claire." Mrs. Miller rose, which woke the little boy. She rushed toward Mrs. Sampson and met her halfway. "Thank you so much for coming. I didn't know who else to call."

"That's what friends are for." The two women hugged. "How is she?"

"She's awake now. We're trying to pull ourselves together, waiting to talk to her doctors again." She glanced in the direction of the man in the suit, who rubbed the back of his neck but said nothing.

"This is Cathy Robichaud, Wendy's mother," Mrs. Sampson said.

"I'm so sorry to learn Tookie's been ill," Mom said. "I hope she'll be all right."

"That's very sweet of you." Mrs. Miller gave Mom a shaky smile.

"What can we do to help, Ann?" Mrs. Sampson asked.

"Tookie would probably like to see the girls. Room 402, over there." Mrs. Miller nodded toward the nurse's station and the stern-faced woman on duty.

Jennifer held my arm in a vise lock. Maybe to keep me from chickening out, but no, her face was white behind her freckles. Like she was about to turn and run.

"What's wrong?" It was the first time I'd ever, *ever* seen Jennifer afraid.

"I don't want to see what she looks like," Jennifer whispered. This from a girl who once forced me to look at a book of eye diseases in her father's office.

"It'll be okay. Come on." I took her hand and we walked together to Tookie's room.

I swallowed hard to settle my stomach again and pushed open the swinging door. The lighting was soft and the room quiet, except for the beeping of a machine. Tookie leaned back against her bed pillows, her face turned toward the windows even though the blinds were closed. Her hair fell in red strings against the shoulders of a faded green hospital gown. An IV dripped fluid into one of her arms. Her body barely made a wrinkle under the bed covers.

"Hi, Tookie," I said gently.

She lay still for a second. Then she turned her head toward us slowly, her eyes only slits, as though it hurt to move. Blue veins showed through her skin, and her lips were so pale they almost disappeared.

"What are you doing here?" she asked.

"We wanted to see you," I said.

"We came to see you," Jennifer said in a voice that was a strange mimic of my own. She stood at my side, her shoulder touching mine.

"Why?" Tookie glared at us. "I don't need you to feel sorry for me."

"No—that's, that's not it at all," I stammered, but in reality it was.

"Oh, then to gloat because your lives are better than mine?" Tookie raised her eyebrows and sat up straighter in the bed.

My life? Was she kidding? Or blind? I shook my head. "To make sure you were all right." I surprised myself by meaning that.

Tookie sighed and looked at Jennifer. "So we're friends now all of a sudden?"

The pink rushed back into Jennifer's face and she took a half step backward.

"We were never *not* friends." Jennifer frowned. "We competed for some of the same things, but that didn't make us enemies."

Tookie shrugged her shoulders. "You know what happened, don't you?" She spoke to no one in particular as she studied the drip in her arm.

"You were starving yourself, and you passed out," I blurted.

Tears collected in her eyes, and she turned toward the windows again.

"The shrink says I try to be perfect, and that's impossible to accomplish." Her voice cracked. "I do, you know, try to be perfect. I try to be the perfect daughter, but my parents are never satisfied. They expect me to look perfect, talk perfect, act perfect, and never make mistakes."

She faced us once more. "I may not look perfect yet, but I'm getting there. I only need to lose a few more pounds."

Her trembling hands grabbed the bed covers and flung them back to expose her legs.

I gasped, and Jennifer's nails dug into my arm.

She looked like someone from a concentration camp. There were no muscles left.

Fifteen

Before morning bell the next day, Jennifer and I paid the Sticks a visit under the oak tree. The mood was all-out misery.

With Tookie gone, Melissa was now the leader. She flipped her glossy black hair behind her shoulders with fingers that had nails chewed down to the quick.

"Hey, Melissa." Jennifer spoke first.

"I don't know anything," Melissa blurted, eyes glassy and lips pale. She started to cry, but in a second, raged at the rest of the herd. "Shut up! I can't even think!" The other Sticks clutched their designer shoulder bags against their bodies as if to shield themselves. Jennifer and I didn't stay long.

The Suaves had deserted the Sticks and stood in a secluded spot against the main building nearby. One buried his hands deep in the pockets of his khakis, in spite of the heat. Another kicked at the dirt in silence. A couple of guys focused on their smart phones, while another leaned against the brick wall with his arms folded.

In homeroom, whispers floated from lips to ears. Notes were passed. David and I locked eyes once. I looked away first. Jennifer didn't talk much, and John-Monster left me alone. Mrs. Perez sat at her desk writing in her journal, except when Miss Carter popped her head in to ask how she was doing.

An announcement blared over the PA system about a special assembly in the gym at nine o'clock. Two psychologists from the Department of Education showed up and gave a PowerPoint presentation about eating disorders. They handed out brochures. Tookie wasn't mentioned. Afterward, they moved to the library to answer questions and give counseling in case anyone wanted to talk about themselves or someone they knew who had a problem.

"Why do you think she did it?" Jennifer asked me. We walked out of the gym and headed back toward homeroom, avoiding the library. Her eyes focused somewhere in the distance, squinting, although gray clouds blocked the sun.

"Better yet, how?" I asked. "I don't eat a lot, but when I'm hungry, I like to eat." I took a chocolate bar from my purse and unwrapped it. I offered her a piece.

She shook her head.

I took a bite and let it melt on my tongue. "I could never deprive myself of food, or force myself to throw up either." I matched her slow pace step by step as we entered our building and proceeded down the hall.

"She wanted to be skinny." Jennifer answered her own question, her voice low and fragile. "She thought skinny looked good, and if she looked good, she'd be a winner."

"A winner of what?"

"Everything—popularity, the cute boys, the part of Laurey."

"Well, I'm skinny, and that hasn't helped me win anything," I said. "I hope one day to be overweight," I added with a grin, but Jennifer didn't laugh. She didn't even look at me.

"Did you know a lot of professional ballet dancers become anorexic or bulimic?" Jennifer had that scared face again, like she had at the hospital.

"Why? Doesn't dancing all day and night keep them slim enough?"

"There's a ton of competition for spots in the ballet companies. When you have very little body fat, your muscles are more pronounced, and your neck and legs appear longer," Jennifer said. "That makes you more desirable as a dancer."

"You're not worried about having to do that, are you?" I didn't want to hear her answer.

"What—starve myself?"

I nodded.

"Yeah, sometimes I am." She spoke in a whisper, then looked away.

"Well, promise me you won't."

No response.

I grabbed her wrist to make her stop walking, and my fingers wrapped all the way around it. They hadn't been able to do that since elementary school. "Look at me and promise."

We both looked from her skinny arm into each other's faces. She opened her mouth, but the words I needed to hear didn't come out.

"Promise me!"

She jerked free of my grasp. "I promise." But her eyes didn't convince me.

A lump settled into my belly with the chocolate.

Sixteen

In spite of everything going on with Jennifer, with me, and *between* Jennifer and me, we managed to find good homes for Chanceaux and her puppies. I couldn't speak for Jennifer, but helping them sure made me forget about myself for the short time I was with them.

My dog, Angel, had been the only pet I'd ever owned, so I didn't have much experience before this. I was surprised all of these dogs had individual personalities just like people do. Jennifer and I used that information to match them with the best owners.

We worked on Mrs. Villaturo, who lived alone, to adopt Chanceaux. They were both gentle and nurturing and would be good company for each other.

"I'll have Chanceaux spayed so she can retire from having puppies," Mrs. V said. "That way, she and I can enjoy retirement together."

We recommended the Nguyen family adopt the most active male puppy. The four Nguyen kids rolled around in the grass with him and let him lick their faces. Their puppy would never be bored or lonely.

We helped Mr. Brown select the brown puppy—we all laughed about the color choice. "Brownie" already acted like the watchdog of the litter, barking any time a stranger came around. He could watch over Mrs. Brown and the twins while Mr. Brown worked at night.

Miss Taylor chose the independent female puppy. "We'll have a great time being two girlfriends who do everything together," she said, placing a new pink collar around her puppy's neck.

Jennifer's grandparents on her father's side needed a dog to live out in the country on their farm. They took the largest male of the litter and named him after the biggest thing they could think of. "Texas" would have a huge place to run and play.

I made all the new owners promise they'd take their puppies to a veterinarian to have them spayed or neutered once they were old enough. I never wanted any of those puppies to make more unwanted babies like they could've if Jennifer and I hadn't helped them.

"I'm very impressed with what you girls have done," Mr. Sampson said, when all but one of the puppies had gone to their new homes.

That was nice of him, but nobody needed to tell me that

Jennifer and I had done a good thing. The puppies' and people's happy faces said it all. And I was pretty happy too. In fact, it filled my soul like Grand-mere Robichaud's gumbo—all warm and satisfying.

Chanceaux's last puppy to be adopted was the timid honey-colored runt of the litter, which had always been my favorite. I took her home with me and named her Belle—French for *beautiful*.

Seventeen

"Wendy, I'm here!" Jennifer let herself into the house.

"Hey, I'm in the kitchen cleaning up."

It was the week before final exams, and we'd planned to get together every afternoon to study. Jennifer had agreed to ride her bike over to my house because I'd ridden over to hers all those days I'd taken care of the puppies.

Yeah, true friendship must have give-and-take like that.

I was up to my elbows in sudsy dishwater when Jennifer walked into the kitchen. Her book bag landed with a thud into one of the chairs at the table.

I half-turned. "I'm almost finished…"

Then I saw her. *Really* saw her. Jennifer's favorite jeans, which once fit so snugly, hung loosely around her hips.

The dish I was rinsing slipped out of my hand and fell to the floor. I didn't even see it as it shattered into a thousand pieces.

All I saw was Jennifer.

"Oh, Wendy! Let me help you."

The mess on the floor came into focus. "Thanks," I said. We both stooped to pick up the largest pieces of porcelain and began dropping them into the trashcan. "One good thing about mismatched garage-sale dishes—it's no big deal when one of them breaks."

"I'll get the broom and dustpan." Jennifer stood up and turned toward the cleaning closet. The difference in her rear end was obvious as the jeans bagged around it.

"Jen, have you lost weight?"

"I don't know." Her voice dragged. "I've been busy with rehearsals and school and my dance classes. Maybe I'm burning more calories." She gave me a look that said *Leave it alone.*

I did, but I'd be sure to pay more attention to how the rest of her clothes fit her in the future.

We settled into my room and plodded through the review guides for each exam subject one at a time, but I couldn't concentrate. Because other things about Jennifer had changed too. The sparkle was gone from her eyes. She didn't laugh at the things I said, at least not as often. And when she did, she didn't bounce.

Maybe she was just as maxed out as I was. That had to be it. After all, I hadn't noticed her losing a whole jean size, I was so busy. How could I expect her to be perky and fun when she had so much to do?

I watched Jennifer's every move, every expression—until

she caught me staring at her like a psycho.

"What!" she demanded. She jutted her jaw forward, showing a perfectly straight bottom row of teeth, and opened her eyes wide.

"Nothing." I shook my head and looked away. I couldn't handle the way she glared at me.

Every hour when we took a break, we made sure to play with Belle. Jennifer still wasn't herself, but she went through the motions, at least.

We played tug-of-war using the knotted cotton rope toy Mrs. V had given Belle after she destroyed a pair of Mom's bedroom slippers. And I had bought a chewie to prevent Belle from chewing on the furniture.

Jennifer and I sat on the floor of my room and took turns hiding the chewie under our shirts. Belle sniffed all over us until she found it. That was one way to get a giggle out of Jennifer.

After a round of play, Belle lapped up a whole bowl of water, so we took her outside for a bathroom break. We sat on the edge of the patio and watched her tiny legs struggle through the grassy jungle.

"Sometimes I wish I were a little puppy like Belle," Jennifer said, her chin resting on crossed arms covering her knees, "and didn't have to worry about what I'd be when I grew up."

"Are you really worried?" Even if the ballerina thing didn't work out, Jennifer had so much going for her. She could be anything she wanted to be.

She shrugged and sighed. "I'd better go before it gets dark."

She lifted herself off the patio.

"But it's only six o'clock." I scrambled to my feet. "I thought you were staying for dinner."

She stretched for a second, and then headed inside. I scooped Belle into my arms and followed.

Jennifer quickly gathered her things from my room. "I'll see you tomorrow."

"Okay." What was the hurry?

In the kitchen, Mom insisted that Jennifer call home before leaving. Another two minutes and she was gone.

Sadness washed over me. I stood on our driveway and watched her ride down the street until I could no longer see the back of her golden head in the evening sunlight.

Eighteen

Nobody really expected to see Tookie again before the end of the school year. A few days later in homeroom, Mrs. Perez announced that Tookie was recuperating and "we all wish her the best." We should consider sending get-well cards if we had her home address. No mention was made of what had actually happened.

Whatever. I was pretty sure everybody in eighth grade already found out she had gone into rehab.

I designed a get-well card with puppies drawn on the front. Inside I wrote, "Thinking of you and hoping you feel like a brand new puppy very soon." I mailed the card to her at the Hickoryhurst Center for Eating Disorders.

I was almost done with my art projects for *Oklahoma*. The surrey and most of the other large props were completed and stood upright in the gym. Amazing volunteer parents had helped by painting a cornfield and some other backdrops.

For the projects I had left, I estimated the hours I had available to work on them. Then I figured out how much time I could allow myself for each piece and wrote that information next to the item on the list. That was the only way I could be sure to finish everything and get my studying and chores at home done too. Organization was my friend. It had to be, living with Mom.

At rehearsals, Jennifer's strong, clear voice rang through the gym. People stopped what they were doing to watch her. Fans appeared almost everywhere she went during the school day, and she always took the time to stop and chat with them. Except for the recent weight loss, she seemed like her old self. What a relief.

The closer we got to performance day, the noisier the gym became, and the harder it was for me to concentrate. Would it have killed anybody to let me break the rules just once and wear earphones? Instead, I had to mentally tune out the sounds from musicians and actors and everyone else buzzing around me.

I kicked off my flats and knelt on the floor to create the pattern for a tree with a barrel in front of it, like Jennifer had suggested.

I had just finished when a person's shadow flickered across the paper. The scent of new leather tickled my nose. My eyes traveled from a pair of black cowboy boots upward. David.

Cast as Curly McLain, the handsome cowboy—and

Jennifer's leading man—David wore blue jeans, a red plaid shirt, and a genuine cowboy hat in light tan felt. He took off the hat and held it in both hands, leaving his curly hair adorably messed up.

The butterflies fluttering inside my chest beat their wings so fast I could hardly breathe.

"Everything looks awesome, Wendy. You're a really good artist." He smiled.

My face warmed. Maybe he was flirting a little. Stupid, he probably missed Tookie. "Thanks," I said.

As he walked away, I groaned under my breath. *That was it? Wendy, you idiot!*

I shook my head. There was no hope of making him like me.

I stood up and began to gather my supplies before leaving for the day. Where were my flats? I looked around, found them, and slipped my right foot into its shoe. Inside the left shoe was a yellow sticky note.

Your art rocks.

A FREND

Nineteen

The last week of school was a ruthless pile-on.

Eighth-graders took their final exams during the first three days of the week. After Jennifer and I finished our exams each day, we were allowed to go back to the gym to work on *Oklahoma.*

By the time I completed my last exam—a grueling one in Science—I felt as ragged as Belle's rope toy after she chewed and dragged it around for a week. My head didn't have room for one more fact or formula. It had closed its doors and locked them down tight, straining with a painful pressure. On autopilot, I trudged over to the gym to work on my few remaining art pieces.

Mixing some paint would help me relax. Anything to do with art always did. I poured a little water into the powdered tempera paint and stirred. Better already. I got down on my knees and dipped a brush into the brown color. I started applying the paint to plywood using long, easy strokes.

A person's shadow fell across my work, but I didn't bother to stop. John-Monster hadn't bullied me since before Tookie's collapse in homeroom, and I was used to people stopping for a second or two to check out my projects. It was probably just another admirer. Unfortunately, not.

"Look at Bird Face," he said, in a singsong voice.

I dropped the paintbrush and squeezed my eyes shut, still on my knees. *Please, not today. Not now. I'm too tired.* I opened my eyes, hoping he would be gone.

John-Monster lingered. The corners of his wide mouth curled upward like on a Halloween mask. What did he want from me?

"You don't actually believe you can be a real *artist.*"

That did it. That was the nastiest thing he could have said to me. I couldn't take any more of his meanness, words like bombs, me running and taking cover, no energy to pretend they didn't hurt me.

"Leave me alone." I tried to steady my voice like for a command, but it came out a weak little chirp.

"Leave me alone," he mimicked. Then he reached for the paintbrush.

"No!" I sprung to my feet and tried to intercept his arm. I couldn't let him sabotage my work again.

He snatched the loaded brush before I could stop him, then held it over his head and out of my reach.

A panic seized me. In spite of the difference in our sizes, I lunged toward him.

He laughed and jerked his arm back, sending a spray of brown paint behind him.

I screamed as the little brown globs arched through the air and landed with a splatter a few yards away—on Jennifer.

John-Monster turned to look, just as Jennifer practically flew at him in a gigantic ballerina leap.

I clapped both hands over my mouth and waited for her to kick the paintbrush right out of his hand.

Instead, she landed between him and me. "What do you think you're doing?" she shrieked. Her face was flushed with rage and covered in brown splotches.

The other students within earshot crept closer to watch our little freak show.

John-Monster turned crimson and stammered, "Uh, nothing." He tossed the paintbrush onto some newspaper spread on the floor.

"What did you call her?" Jennifer stepped forward and confronted him toe-to-toe. For a definition of "in your face," this was it.

His glance shifted from one of us to the other.

I was somewhat confused myself. Was she mad at him for splattering her with paint—or for bullying me?

"Wasn't it 'Bird Face'?" She persisted, emphasizing the last two words. I was mortified. Everyone's eyes were on me now, the ugly bird-face girl. Everything around me spun into a blur as I stood in the spotlight of this horrible little drama. *David, please don't be in the crowd watching this.*

"No." John-Monster studied the floor.

"Liar!" Jennifer's eyes blazed. A vein bulged from her forehead. Her hands curled into fists.

John-Monster snapped to attention.

Was she going to punch him? She'd get kicked out of school if I didn't do something. I mustered some courage and whispered, "It's okay, Jen."

She ignored me and turned to the crowd. "You've heard him say it before, haven't you?"

Several of the spectators nodded. One female voice said, "Yes."

"Apologize to her," Jennifer demanded of John-Monster through clenched teeth.

Surrounded by a group apparently sympathetic to his victim, he caved. I guess it was one thing to pick on a skinny girl who couldn't defend herself or to have a shouting match with her best friend, but to face a mob? He fidgeted with his glasses and swallowed hard.

"I'm sorry," he said to me in a flat tone.

I looked at him but said nothing.

Mr. Stanley, who'd been playing his cello with the student orchestra, headed our way. John-Monster turned and disappeared.

Jennifer stood at my side, breathing through her mouth as her face returned to its normal color.

My hands trembled. I couldn't decide whether to hug her or hit her. I picked up a wet rag and handed it to her so she could wipe away the paint.

For the first time in our lives, I was not grateful that Jennifer had rescued me.

Sitting in the back of the bus on the way home, Jennifer looked me square in the eyes and blurted, "Wendy, you need to stop acting like a Bird Face."

"What?" Unbelieving, I stared at her. I didn't do anything wrong!

With earnest eyes and a soft tone, she said, "I know you're shy, but you're such a great person, and more people need to know that. You're the best friend I've ever had, and you think I have good taste, don't you?"

I chuckled in spite of myself.

"If you would try a little harder to talk to other people…" she suggested gently.

I bit my lip.

"…and to show that you're friendly…"

I shrugged.

"…then it wouldn't be so easy for people like John to get to you."

I shook my head. Why should I be the one to change?

"When you can talk to people about what's on your mind, no matter what it is, you'll be able to stand up for yourself when you need to," she said.

I looked away and squinted to fight back tears.

"Not that I minded telling John off this time." She touched

my arm.

I blinked a few times while digging tissues from my bag, then blew my nose.

Jennifer didn't say anything else for the rest of the ride home. I guessed she finally knew when to stop talking.

When I dumped the used tissues from my purse that night, a crumpled yellow sticky note fell out—the one I'd hidden from Jennifer at lunchtime a few weeks earlier.

Be strong.

A FREND

I took a deep breath and squared my shoulders. Did I have what it took to go from wimp to Wonder Woman? I slumped again.

Baby steps.

The next morning I made it a point to find Alice. Technically, all eighth-graders were out of school and wouldn't report back until Monday for report cards. But I needed to finish painting one of my art pieces, and Alice still had to rehearse with the orchestra.

"Alice!" I trotted up behind her at the bottom of the stage.

She turned, clarinet in hand. "Hey." Her pink cheeks grew scarlet.

"I was wondering if you were available for a little while."

"Um, sure, we're taking a break now."

"I'd like your opinion on some paint colors. Would you

mind?"

Surprise flashed in her eyes. "No, not at all."

"Great! Thanks."

She placed her clarinet in its case by her chair and closed the lid.

"How's practice going?" I asked, as we walked toward my project area.

"Good. We're working on synchronizing the music."

"Oh. Great." I didn't have a clue as to what she was talking about.

Alice smiled. "Come watch us when you get a chance."

We arrived at my paint stand and stood in front of an unfinished piece.

"What do you think of this green?" I held up a sample board.

"It's nice, but…"

"Really, tell me what you think."

Surprisingly, a quiet girl like her could talk a blue streak once you got her going.

When the time was right, I'd work the topic of skin care into a conversation.

Twenty

The Spring Program took place the last Friday night of the school year.

Overnight, the gym transformed into an auditorium with enough folding chairs to seat several hundred people. Gold-colored curtains now hid the stage. Black cables for lighting and sound systems snaked below it.

Families arrived early. They surrounded Mom and me and the two extra seats we were saving. While adults visited with one another, kids ran around and knocked chairs out of line. The basketball coaches must've been having a fit over the shoes and chair legs scraping across their precious floor.

Speaking of legs, mine looked pretty good, so I wore a skirt, one a little shorter than the school dress code allowed. Nobody would take a measurement tonight. I pulled my crucifix out from under my top for a second but dropped it back inside again.

Mom and I had invited Mrs. Villaturo to be our guest. She arrived wearing a suit and gloves like she was going to a wedding or something. At least she didn't wear a hat. Anyway, I was glad to have someone there who could pass for my grandmother.

Dad hadn't responded to my letter. No big surprise. Maybe it was better that way, at least for Mom's sake. I had told her about the letter, which might have been a mistake. Her wrist braces were gone, and she had bought a new dress and gone to a salon to have her hair done. Her eyes searched the crowd continuously, and she turned around a couple of times at the sound of a man's voice. As the gym filled with people, I got tired of saying "This seat is taken" and finally gave up saving one for Dad.

When the lights went down and the curtains parted to reveal the student symphony, the audience gasped in appreciation. I hardly recognized some of the kids. Wearing black suits and dresses, they sat at attention better than they'd ever done in class, their eyes focused on the conductor. The boys' hair was washed and combed—even stinky Eddie Andrew's. Some of the girls had styled their hair up with black barrettes or bows, and a few wore jewelry that glittered from their ears or around their necks. Instruments gleamed under the lights as everyone performed Pachelbel's *Canon in D Major*, my favorite piece of classical music.

Next on the program, Frank Chawlk and his younger brother delivered a stand-up comedy routine that was hilarious. They were followed by a singing duet from a seventh-grade girl and her talking parrot. Mom never laughed so hard.

Dad still wasn't there. I needed to just forget about him.

Now *Oklahoma*.

Mom pointed to my name listed under "Set Design" on the playbill. "I'm so proud of you." She hugged me tight.

The show opened with David, as Curly, singing "Oh, What a Beautiful Mornin'." From the third row, Mom and I scanned the stage, and I pointed out my favorite works in the scene. "Everything looks great," she said.

Mrs. Villaturo smiled and squeezed my hand. "Good job, Wendy."

The curtains closed for a minute and reopened with changes of a few props and pieces of scenery.

Jennifer entered the stage wearing a pink and white gingham dress, her hair pulled back and up from the sides with a huge white bow. She oozed goodness and warmth. Was it just the stage lights, or was she actually glowing? I'd swear there was a halo around her head. The audience watched her every move as though she had one, too. Perfectly beautiful, she spoke and sang and moved across the stage without a single mistake in her performance, as far as I could tell.

Actually, she seemed to be having the time of her life—the life I would've given anything to own. David drew close to her side and took her hand in his. He smiled his great big beautiful smile at her, and she returned one right back at him. Then she and David sang, "People Will Say We're in Love," and they stared into each other's eyes like they really meant it.

Blood rushed to my face. *That witch!* Had she liked David

all this time—and she hid it from me? Of course! She suspected I liked him. She had thousands of chances to be near him. She knew she wouldn't have to do anything to get him. She just had to look like Jennifer.

All of a sudden, nothing else mattered—not my talent or accomplishments or the praise I'd received. Everything and everyone else in the auditorium disappeared before my eyes. There was only Jennifer and David.

Thoughts crashed against one another inside my head. *Why couldn't I be the one up there with David? Why couldn't I be the one who was lucky enough to be born so pretty that everybody liked me? Why couldn't I take ballet lessons and have two parents to give me everything I ever wanted?*

I gritted my teeth and wadded the hem of my skirt in my fists.

This wasn't fair! Nobody tried harder than me to always do the right thing. Nobody worked harder than I did to help people who needed me. Nobody prayed harder to have a father who acted like he cared. What did all that effort get me? Nothing! The only things that mattered were being pretty and popular. I wasn't either one, so all I could expect was to be ridiculed or bullied—or completely ignored.

A scream rose in my throat. Only holding my breath kept it from escaping.

I'd thought I could handle the way things were, like it was part of some divine plan, but I couldn't handle jack. I was sick of it. All of it. All of them!

I hated God for making me the way he did and for making Pete Robichaud my father.

I wanted to slap David across his stupid smiling face for making me like him so much.

I wanted to strangle Jennifer for being so pretty and perfect.

I wanted Jennifer to—to *fail*.

Fail? I sat up straight. Did I really mean that?

Yes, *fail* at something for a change! Anything. Now would be a good time. Sing off-key, slip and fall, cough, sneeze—something. Make a mistake!

But she didn't even let go of David's hand long enough to scratch her nose.

A burst of applause and an ear-splitting whistle jolted me back to reality. Then came a standing ovation. I folded my arms tight across my chest and refused to get up. Why did I even bother coming here tonight—to this adoration-fest for Jennifer? I wanted to throw up.

Mom looked at me funny. "Are you all right?"

"Yeah." I unfolded my arms and forced out a few claps. I didn't stand. I should have, but I couldn't make myself do it.

The curtains closed, then reopened a few seconds later. The players took their final bows. When the curtains closed once again, I took a deep breath and rose from my seat on shaky legs.

"Thank you so much for inviting me," Mrs. Villaturo said. "I had a wonderful time." She hugged Mom and kissed me on the cheek.

"It was our pleasure," Mom said.

"I'll leave you two to linger and visit with your friends."
Mrs. Villaturo smiled at me. "Good night."

I forced a smile in return. "Good night, Mrs. V."

She turned and walked toward the side exit.

Mom and I joined the crowd moving down the center aisle.
Mr. and Mrs. Sampson had sat a couple of rows behind ours
and waited for us to reach them. Their faces beamed, and Mr.
Sampson carried a red rose.

"Congratulations on the fine artwork, Wendy Robichaud,"
Mr. Sampson said.

I cringed at the French accent.

Mrs. Sampson wrapped an arm around me and patted my
shoulder. "Very nice," she said. "You're on your way to an art
career, young lady."

"Thank you."

At that moment I spotted Jennifer running toward us at full
speed, the skirt of her long blue dress from the closing act hiked
up to her knees.

She grinned from ear to ear and began to squeal when she
got within a few yards of us. "Did you like it?" she asked, before
she had completely stopped, flushed and nearly breathless.

"Oh, yes, very much," Mom said. "Congratulations on your
performance."

"You were great, Jen!" Mr. Sampson handed Jennifer the
rose and kissed her on the forehead.

Mrs. Sampson gave her a huge hug. "You were wonderful,
sweetie."

I stood still and didn't say anything. Jennifer turned to me, smiling, with an expectant look on her face.

"It was okay." My comment chilled the air. I was the ice queen of Bellingrath.

An invisible eraser removed the happiness from Jennifer's face. Left was the same look of uncertainty Chanceaux had the first time I saw her.

I'd never before hurt Jennifer on purpose. Immediately, I wanted to say something to reverse that look on her face—one sweet word was all it would take—but my bitter insides could not produce one.

Mom studied me and pursed her lips. "It's been a long day. We'd better be getting home." She nudged my arm.

"Good night," Mr. and Mrs. Sampson said in unison, their eyebrows raised.

Mom's laser-beam eyes bore into the side of my face as we walked away. I refused to look at her, afraid I might reveal what lay deep in my soul.

If I said out loud what I'd hoped would happen to Jennifer, then my hateful thought might take form and come alive. If Jennifer failed at something she loved, she wouldn't be the same Jennifer I knew. It was bad enough I couldn't forgive myself for wishing for her failure, but if it became a reality, it would mean the death of us. Together, Jennifer and I would never be the same.

We exited through the doors of the gym into the night air thick with a low-lying fog. The man in the moon high above us smirked at me.

Mom broke the silence. "Wendy, there's your father."

Under the eerie glow of the lights at the opposite edge of the parking lot Dad stood, wearing a blazer and tie. Any other time, I might not have recognized him. But Margaret, Michael, and Christopher were with him.

I stopped dead in my tracks. Well, wasn't that just *great*.

"You go talk to them, and I'll wait here," Mom said. She nodded and waved cordially to them across the distance.

I dragged myself in the direction of where they waited, all four of them smiling and looking a whole lot happier than I must have looked.

Maybe I should have been glad to see Dad. He obviously had made some effort. But I wasn't in the mood to see anyone—particularly his whole other family, and especially since I had invited only him. And what nerve he had to show up at the end like that, with no notice whatsoever.

The closer I got to him, the clearer his face became, and I hated that face. Disappointment turned into anger, and the angrier I became, the faster my legs moved. I reached him in a few seconds.

My face burned, spewing words too hot to be contained any longer. "Where *were* you?" I yelled at Dad, ignoring Margaret and the boys. "I've been waiting all night!"

"We were sitting in the back. I guess you didn't see us."

"You should have called to let me know you were coming." Blood rushed again to my head until I thought it might explode.

"And you should have sat with me."

The smile fell off Dad's face. "You should be glad we came."

"Oh, am I supposed to be grateful every time you feel like showing up but never say anything when you don't?" My hands cut the air like a double karate chop and landed with a slap against my thighs. "Thanks for nothing."

I turned and stomped back toward the gym.

So in one night I pretty much drove away everyone I cared about, except Mom.

Good job, Wendy.

Twenty-one

I sat in my beanbag chair Saturday morning, arms crossed, and kicked at a big wrinkle in the carpet with the heel of my shoe until the fibers started coming loose.

The worst part was that I'd screwed up what would have been the best weekend of the school year since spring break. Mom had fully recovered, so my household chores had returned to normal. Chanceaux and the puppies had all gone to good homes. I'd made it through final exams, and my work for the Spring Program was complete—and a huge success. Summer vacation would start as soon as Jennifer and I received our report cards on Monday.

According to our plan, Jennifer and I would've been at Skate-abration all day, and tonight we were supposed to bake chocolate chip cookies and stuff ourselves until we hurt. We'd write fan letters to our favorite recording artists and ask for autographed pictures to give us something to look forward to in the mail all summer long.

Instead, the day stretched ahead of me like a thousand miles of barren desert. Complete with scorpions.

At the least little sound outside my window, I leapt out of my chair to check and see if Jennifer had ridden up on her bike. Each time the phone rang, I listened to Mom's side of the conversation and hoped it was Jennifer on the other end of the line.

If she was upset by the way I'd acted—if? Ha! Tookie couldn't have been more rude to her than I was.

I dragged the beanbag chair over the shabby spot in the carpet and began to pace the room. Jennifer probably expected an apology. But why should I? Everything always had to be about *her*. She would just have to get over it and come around.

I refused an offer of French toast for breakfast, pretending not to feel well. That way, Mom would call Dad and tell him I'd be skipping the usual Sunday afternoon visit the next day. I wasn't about to apologize for what I'd said to him, and I certainly wasn't up to dealing with my stepmother or stepbrothers either.

At lunchtime I ate a small amount of the homemade chicken soup Mom always made when she thought I was sick. I put up with getting my temperature taken every few hours rather than explain to her what was really bugging me—guilt.

It overwhelmed me. How could I have been so mean to Jennifer? It wasn't her fault she was good-looking. David would have to be blind not to notice. What was wrong with me? I always thought I was a good person, and there was no doubt

Jennifer was a great person. She was my best friend—my only real friend. Hadn't she always been there for me?

Sweet memories of our friendship flooded my mind:

Jennifer waiting for me to finish my chores, when she could have called someone else to come to her house.

Jennifer helping to care for Chanceaux and the puppies because she knew that's what I wanted to do.

Jennifer laughing at my stupid jokes and making me laugh when I took myself too seriously.

Jennifer complimenting me on my drawings, my English compositions, my hair.

Jennifer offering to share everything she owned with me.

Jennifer protecting me from John-Monster.

And I had ruined it all.

Twenty-two

I skipped church Sunday morning. I needed to convince Mom that I still didn't feel well, so the bags under my eyes from lack of sleep helped. The clincher was not taking a shower. I'd have to endure my own grunge all day, but I couldn't take a chance she'd change her mind and make me go to Dad's.

I cracked my door open and poked my head around as Mom walked by. "I don't think I'm any better today."

She squinted at my face and dirty hair. "Get back into bed." She frowned and took my temperature again.

Lying next to me, Belle watched as I dumped the contents of my backpack onto the center of the bedspread. I was determined to do away with all reminders of the Spring Program, David, John-Monster, and the whole crummy mess of the last two months. Starting with the big stuff, I tossed the *Oklahoma* playbill into the wastebasket, along with my projects list, the exam review sheets, and some notebooks. Among the hair brush, lip balm, and packs of gum remaining in the pile were all the yellow sticky-note messages.

Could there have been so many in the last several weeks? Smoothing out the wrinkles, I flattened and lined them up. I counted seven.

Nice face.

Only words.

Be strong.

Good luck.

Speak up.

It's his problem.

Your art rocks.

I stared at the little slips of yellow and sighed. Those few words held a lot of support and encouragement. But who could the author be? I scraped my fingernails through my greasy scalp, pulling my hair when I got to the ends. *Aaargh!*

I swiped my hand across the bedspread, sending the little squares into the air like yellow butterflies. Who had time to play detective? I'd been too busy, and time was running out. If somebody in eighth grade had written the notes, he—or she—might not continue to the public high school with me. A Catholic high school sat on the next block down from the church, and a private school was located on the other side of town. I might never know who cared so much about me. Add that to the looooong list of disappointments in my pathetic life. My shoulders slumped, and I flung myself backward onto the bed. Would it always be like this?

Lying on my back with my feet dangling, I stared at the ceiling. Clusters of water spots formed hideous faces on the white surface, and they glared back at me mockingly. I covered my own face with a pillow and held it until I felt lost in a sea of blackness.

What did my secret friend see when he looked at me anyway? For some reason, I hoped it was a "he." Ugh. If he thinks *I'm* attractive, he must be a real pig. I started mentally listing all the ugly boys at school, but the field was too wide. I released the pillow and got up, walked over to the dresser and studied my face in the mirror.

Humph. I couldn't do anything about the way I looked on the outside, but the outside never mattered to Jennifer. *Jennifer.* My heart ached.

On my bulletin board was a photo taken of us at the Aquarium of the Americas, our arms around each other. I missed her. Maybe I should apologize. Or maybe not. She wouldn't expect to see me on a Sunday anyway. And by tomorrow everything would probably be back to normal. I'd wait.

I smoothed my hair with both hands and faced the mirror again. Jennifer, John-Monster, and the sticky-note writer—they all saw something different.

I turned my head to the left, cutting my eyes to the right as I ran the index finger of my left hand down the slope of my nose. So what if my face wasn't perfect? Having a pretty face hadn't helped Tookie feel any better about herself. And Jennifer's good looks, along with all the other things she had going for her, weren't keeping her from worrying about the future.

Nice face.

Maybe my face could be considered nice enough—and possibly even friendly, if I worked at it. I forced a smile. That was better.

But I couldn't go around smiling like an idiot all the time. I needed to vocalize, to say the things I often thought about saying—sometimes too late. Where did I hear something like that before? Oh, yeah. Jennifer.

She tried to tell me. Now I wanted to kick myself for all the chances I'd missed with David. Jennifer probably knew I would. I kicked the beanbag chair instead.

And what about letting John-Monster walk all over me? If it hadn't been him tormenting me, it would have been somebody else eventually. I was an easy target. Just like Jennifer said. Why did she always have to be right?

I never thanked her for that little talk she gave me on the bus. But I was finally catching on. Except now, I might have to go it alone. I needed self-confidence—and fast. Only problem was, how could I get some? It certainly wasn't on aisle two next to the purple eye shadow. Hey, maybe I could fake it, like I did with the surrey. An illusion was as good as the real thing as long as people believed it, right?

I straightened my shoulders and lifted my chin. "Hello, my name is Wendy," I said aloud to my reflection in the mirror. It came off as more snooty than self-confident. This was going to take some practice. I shook off and composed my face again.

"Which high school are you going to in the fall?" I tilted my head as if waiting for an answer. Okay, I'm in control. I'm the kind of person anyone would want to talk to.

I pretended to be the other person and said, "I just moved here, and I don't know my new school yet."

"Oh, where did you move from?" I asked.

"Houston," I answered my reflection.

"Tell me about Houston," I said, imitating Jennifer's technique.

Good thing the door to my room was already shut—Mom probably thought I was taking a nap—because I would have died if anybody had seen what I was doing. I locked it, just in case.

I created more imaginary scenarios and conversations, trying on facial expressions that exuded confidence. I practiced each conversation until I was certain I wouldn't put my foot in my mouth and insult someone. Or clam up when the going got tough. Like I did with poor Alice. She could really use some emotional support. I wanted to make her feel better—to say the kinds of things that came naturally to Jennifer. Alice needed a compliment. It would have to be a real compliment, though. Not a fake one like Tookie's.

"Your shirt is cute," I said. "That color works great with your hair." Alice would like that, I'd bet.

Okay, getting there. But it would take some pretty good acting to pull off such a drastic change in my personality. Going over the *Oklahoma* script with Jennifer might pay off.

"Oh, hi, Melissa. What are you doing at the mall?" I pretended to ask the Tookie wannabe.

"Well, duh! Shopping, of course," I answered as Melissa.

I let out a huge laugh, startling Belle. She leapt to her feet.

"Yeah, the summer sales are great, aren't they?" I responded as Wendy. Clever comeback. I'd ignore Melissa's rudeness. She'd be speechless. "I'd better get back to it, if I want to get all of my shopping done," I said in a playful tone. "See ya."

That was all very nice, but this wasn't really about me being able to make small talk with a Stick.

What about John-Monster?

"Yeah, I'm talking to *you*." I pointed at myself in the mirror. "I don't know what your problem is," I said, scowling, "but if you don't like the way I look, or you just don't like me at all, then you don't have to talk to me." I made a smirky face. "Who needs you, anyway? There are plenty of other people in the world." I placed both fists on my hips. "Oh, and by the way, have you looked in a mirror lately?"

Take that, John-Monster.

Yeah, that's what I'd do. I'd look him square in the eye and tell him off the very next time I saw him. I practiced a cold, steady gaze until I thought I had it exactly right. *John-Monster, just try to hurt me again. Just try.* I promised myself I wouldn't let anyone get away with calling me names like he had. And I wouldn't look the other way when somebody treated an innocent person badly either, especially a nice person like Alice.

I could do this. I could talk to strangers and defend myself against people like John-Monster. But the thought of talking to my dad or stepmother about anything that really mattered made me shiver.

Twenty-three

Monday. Report Card Day. And I was all practiced up. I wouldn't get dumped on today. Not by John-Monster or anybody else.

Mom dropped off the new and improved Wendy Robichaud right in front of Bellingrath Junior High. No sneaking up the side street to avoid the Sticks. I wore the dress I'd wasted on Dad a few weeks earlier. My gold crucifix rested against its front.

I strutted into my building with a self-assurance that rivaled that of the Suaves. "Hi," I said to each and every eighth-grader I saw—receiving stares, gaping mouths, and a few times, a "Hey" in return. Even from Melissa.

"Have a good summer," I said to everyone else I met, no matter which grade or whether I knew them or not.

Dead ahead was homeroom. I lifted my chin and my chest too, such as it was. *Just you wait, John-Monster.*

I crossed through the doorway, and I was in control. Like when I roller-bladed at full speed. I could change direction whenever I wanted to, but instead I'd yell for everyone to get out of my way—and they did. I would do the same thing with John-Monster. And I would finally stop the pain he caused me. *Look out, John-Monster. I'm your worst nightmare.*

Was that—? My back stiffened, ready for a confrontation, but it wasn't him. Just another tall guy visiting from a different class. Where was John-Monster? Planning a sneak attack?

I worked my way through the room. No sign of him, not even at his desk. *Rats!* Maybe his family took an early vacation. And just when I had a plan. That figured.

A few parents had brought in the usual party junk: cake, chips, dip. While we filled our plates and ate, a lot of kids exchanged phone numbers and addresses or dropped photographs on one another's desks.

I received another yellow sticky-note.

Feeling better?

A FREND

I swung around to find the culprit, but it was like searching for a single ant while the whole colony scurried around. More students from other classes had shown up too, and that made it even harder.

I growled, wadded the note and slammed it to the floor, then squashed it with my shoe. *Stop weirding me out!*

What kind of friend wouldn't have the decency to reveal himself, not even on the last day of school? I squinted like Arnold

Schwarzenegger and scanned the room, trying to read the faces. Would I have to go all summer without knowing who he was?

"Maybe we'll have some classes together in the fall." David eased into an empty desk next to mine and took a bite of cake, leaving a smudge of icing near the corner of his mouth.

"Sure, we probably will," I said, unable to tear my gaze away from the smudge.

"But I should see you before then, like at church."

I nodded and opened my mouth to speak, but my attention was diverted again. A mix of squeals, shouts, and moans rose as Mrs. Perez began to distribute report cards. She walked over and handed ours to David and to me.

Not bad. A's in English, geography, Louisiana history. Science, B-minus. Nice. B in math. Expected, but wouldn't have made it without Jennifer's help. Mom would congratulate me like always. Dad would ask why I'd gotten the B's before even mentioning the A's.

"David, what did you…?" He was gone.

I sighed and stuck the report card in my backpack, then got up and snagged another piece of cake. Chocolate, my favorite.

It was finally time to test my new skills. "Frank, what are you doing this summer?" I smiled, then took a bite of cake and waited. Not so hard.

The color of Frank's face changed from its normal white to the brightest shade of pink.

I stifled a giggle.

He glanced over his shoulder like he thought I was playing

a joke on him. "Um, my brother and I are going to that drama camp at the Little Theatre."

"That sounds cool. Hope you like it."

He grinned.

You actually did it, Wendy.

I moved on, and it got easier each time. Maybe the last day of school had something to do with it. Could have. Everyone acted like they were in a good mood, laughing and talking all at once, stuffing their faces. They practically bounced around the room. In all the excitement, it was easy to avoid getting into a conversation with Jennifer. Was she avoiding me too?

Things quieted down as the party broke up. I had to talk to Mrs. Perez, to tell her goodbye. She'd made homeroom as good as it could be, considering. "I hope you have a good vacation, Mrs. Perez."

She offered me a tight-lipped smile instead of her usual wide grin. "You too, Wendy. You've earned it." Tiny red lines streaked through the whites of her eyes.

Teachers got tired by the end of the school year too, didn't they? Before I had a chance to ask if anything was wrong, Gayle Freeman walked up. She was even more of a mess than usual.

"Excuse us, Wendy, will you please?" Mrs. Perez put her arm around Gayle's shoulders and whispered something to her.

Okay, I knew when I wasn't wanted. There weren't many people left in the room anyway, and the buses were lined up and waiting.

I grabbed my purse and was about to leave when a gentle

hand touched my arm. *Jennifer.*

"Let's go someplace where we can talk," she said.

"All right." I followed her to a quiet area of the schoolyard.

Without hesitation, she turned to me and said, "I'm going to New York."

Something choked me, but it was my own hand on my throat. "What do you mean?" *Please don't say it, don't say it. Don't take this summer away.*

She spoke hurriedly, as though afraid to tell me and wanting to get it all out before she changed her mind. "For a ballet workshop. I'll live with my aunt. She helped my mom get me in."

I wasn't certain I was still breathing.

"I didn't know for sure until Saturday," she continued. "They waited until then because they didn't want to distract me while so much else was going on. We had a lot to talk about. That's why I didn't call or come over."

I took a deep breath and swallowed hard. "When are you leaving?"

"This week. Wednesday."

My heart dove to my stomach. "No! That's the day after tomorrow!"

Our summer together said goodbye and slipped completely out of sight. I had taken it for granted, even while I envied her. How stupid. Now the best thing about summer—Jennifer— would be gone. I turned away so she wouldn't see my eyes filling with tears.

She placed her hand on my arm again and forced me to look

at her. "Wendy, it's only temporary," she said, with a hopeful lilt to her voice. "I'll be back in time for school next fall." In spite of her own optimistic words, tears welled up in her eyes too.

Her reasoning didn't help. She was abandoning me. Maybe I deserved that. Was I being punished for the terrible things I'd been thinking about her? I only hoped she hadn't been able to sense them.

"Jen, I'm sorry I've been acting so weird lately." I pulled tissues from my purse for both of us.

"It's okay. You've had a lot to handle, especially with John and everything." She dabbed her eyes.

"I don't know what I'll do without you all summer."

"You'll do great. I'm the one who can't do anything for herself." She smiled as she touched my hand.

She was trying to make me feel better, of course. Just like always. I smirked and shook my head. We laughed through our tears.

"I promise I'll write to you as soon as I get to New York," she said.

"You mean a real letter on paper?" My favorite kind. "No e-mail?"

She laughed. "Yeah, a real letter. My aunt doesn't have a computer at home."

"Will you send me some pictures too? I've never been there."

"Sure, and I'll tell you about everything I do this summer."

"So will I." If I could make the summer interesting without her, that is.

"You'd better."

"I promise."

Neither of us spoke a single solitary word on the bus ride home. True friendship must have give-and-take like that.

I paced the floor waiting for Mom to get home from work. When she finally stepped through the door, I ran to her and spilled my guts about Jennifer leaving.

"This is probably the first of many times when the two of you will go your separate ways." She stroked my cheek. "But parting will get easier, dear. I promise."

"I'll miss her so much, Mom. I'm not sure I can stand it." I wanted to cry again. The thought of being apart from Jennifer for so long, and by so many miles—it was unbearable. I'd been afraid of destroying us, but I never considered we might disintegrate one day anyway.

Mom wrapped her arms around me in that special kind of hug she used the day of the divorce. The one that made me feel safe—back then. "I know, honey, and I'm sorry."

For the next two days, Jennifer and I spent every spare minute together. I even helped her pack. We boxed up clothes from her closet that she was sure she wouldn't need anymore.

"Wear these and knock 'em dead, girl!" She shoved the box into my arms. "If you sit home all summer not doing anything, I'll be mad at you."

"I'll try."

"No! I want to see pictures of you in these clothes, and you'd better be doing something fun in them."

"Okay, okay." I knew better than to argue with her.

The day she left, I hugged her a long time, hanging on, trying to memorize the smell of her freshness, like new grass in springtime.

"I'll miss you," she said, squeezing me so tight I could hardly breathe. "Kiss Belle for me."

My reply drowned in my throat like a baby's gurgle.

She stepped into the car, and the Sampson family drove away, headed toward New York, on the first Wednesday in June.

Jennifer and I waved at each other until I no longer saw her golden head in the rear window.

That night I lay in bed with my knees drawn up and my arms wrapped around them. With each guttural sound I made, Belle snuggled closer to me, her gentle brown eyes searching my face for a sign that everything was going to be all right. I wasn't sure it would.

Twenty-four

What a lame summer it started out to be with Jennifer gone.

As I rode my bike up and down the block the next morning, I tortured myself with thoughts of what we could've been doing if she hadn't gone to New York. It took every ounce of willpower not to ride all the way to her street, to her empty house, just to see something that was part of her.

Why did I act like such a blockhead? Not showing her nearly enough appreciation while I had her around. My best friend for more than seven years, and I almost threw it all away.

Somewhere between Mr. Brown's house and Miss Taylor's, the truth hit me so hard I nearly fell off the bike.

Maybe it wasn't that I "almost" threw it all away. Maybe Jennifer didn't forgive me for the way I'd acted after the Spring Program. She said it was "okay" when I apologized, but she'd made the decision to go to New York two days before that.

Maybe she wouldn't have chosen to go if I hadn't been such a jerk.

My heart sank like a brick. I might as well have handed her a ticket to leave.

And David—why did I think she wanted to steal him from me? He was never mine to steal in the first place. Now Jennifer would spend the whole summer in New York, I wouldn't get any closer to being with David, and I had to start from scratch in the friendship department. Did I even deserve any friends?

Mrs. Villaturo came out of her house. "Good morning, Wendy." She glanced slong the street. "Jennifer isn't with you? Is she on vacation?"

"No." I passed her and made a U-turn in the street, stopping when I reached her yard again. "She's in New York all summer for a ballet workshop."

"Oh, I see." Her eyes traveled across my face as she pouted her lips. "Why don't you and Belle come over and visit Chanceaux and me?"

"Okay."

"Any time you like."

"Thanks, Mrs. V."

"Are you hungry? If you come in right now, I'll fix you a bacon and egg sandwich."

"That sounds good, thanks." The bike ride had worked off my breakfast cereal.

"Has your mother gone back to work?"

"Yes, ma'am."

"Then you should spend the whole day with me sometime."

That was the best invitation of the summer so far. The next day Belle and I went to Mrs. Villaturo's house. She baked some delicious chocolate chip cookies, and I ate almost a dozen by myself. Although Belle and Chanceaux begged for some too, we didn't give them any because chocolate is bad for dogs. We fed them pieces of cheese instead.

"I think I'd like to do what you and Jennifer did." Mrs. Villaturo stroked Belle's ears as the puppy sat in her lap.

"What do you mean?"

"Take care of a litter of abandoned puppies."

"I know exactly who you need to talk to." Jennifer and I had put our names on a list to volunteer for a local animal rescue organization—one of our many plans for the summer.

A few days later, Mrs. V and I visited the facility and signed up together as volunteers. We'd help rescue dogs like Mrs. V helped rescue me.

Twenty-five

Still, the first weeks of summer dragged. As hard as she tried, Mrs. V couldn't take the place of Jennifer. In an act of desperation, I invited Alice to spend a day with me.

Her voice squeaked with excitement on the phone, and she wanted to come over right after breakfast on Saturday. Awfully eager, but okay.

She arrived at nine sharp. Alice, her father, and five-year-old brother Adam got out of the car and came up the walk together.

Mom beat me to the door.

With one large hand on Adam's shoulder, Mr. Rend extended the other to Mom. His handsome face broke into a huge smile, flushing pink against his blonde hair.

"Hello, I'm Daniel Rend. This is Alice, and this young man is Adam."

"Hi, I'm Cathy. It's so nice to meet you." Mom took Mr.

Rend's hand and giggled. *Giggled.* "Please come in."

Mr. Rend, keeping Adam close by his side, followed Mom into the kitchen.

Alice and I hung out in the living room. I tried to pay attention to Alice while straining for glimpses of Mom and Mr. Rend. They drank coffee and chatted, voices comfortable, laughter light and easy. I breathed a sigh of relief.

About fifteen minutes later, Mr. Rend came out of the kitchen with Adam. Mom smiled as she followed him.

"Alice, I'll pick you up around four." Mr. Rend stroked Alice's hair. "Thanks, Cathy."

"Any time," Mom said.

Mr. Rend loaded Adam into the car and drove away.

Still smiling, Mom wandered back to the kitchen.

I let Belle inside from the backyard. She sniffed around everywhere the Rends had been and then allowed Alice to scratch her neck—her favorite spot. She followed Alice and me to my room.

My plan was in place. I'd purposely left my bottle of acne lotion dead center on the dresser next to some cotton balls so Alice might notice it. Sure enough, she spotted it.

When she lifted her eyebrows in interest, I picked it up and said, "This stuff works great." I applied some to my face. "Want to try it?"

"Yes, thanks." Alice started rubbing the lotion onto her skin with a cotton ball and talking full speed at the same time.

After their mother died in a car accident, Alice and Adam

had spent a few months in a foster home because Mr. Rend was in the Air Force and had to go back overseas for a while. He soon chose to leave the Air Force permanently and come back home to take care of them. Alice, her father, and brother moved to Louisiana, to our town, for a fresh start. They received family counseling right after that.

Counseling. *Hmm.* Maybe it could help Dad be a better father. "What was counseling like?"

"We talked a lot to the counselor, first individually, and then as a family." She laid the used cotton ball on the dresser.

"What about?" I sat on the edge of my bed.

"Oh, lots of things—growing up, missing our dad when he was away, things we remembered about our mother. Anything we wanted to say."

"Didn't you feel funny talking to a stranger about stuff like that?"

"Well, a little at first. But you'd be surprised by the families we saw in the waiting room."

"What fam—?" I stopped to steady myself when she plopped down on the bed next to me and changed the subject.

"You know, I tried out for the high school track team and didn't make it," she said, "but I plan to try out again if there are any spots still open."

"Good idea." I didn't ask why Alice didn't make the team the first time. She had to have seen what happened to me at tryouts, and it was nice of her not to say anything about it.

"Was foster care bad?"

"It wasn't as bad as you might think. At least my brother and I got to stay together, and we knew Dad was coming to get us as soon as he could."

"I'm glad."

"Besides, my foster mother taught me how to knit."

"Cool."

"Knitting is a lot of fun. There are so many interesting kinds of yarns. Some are fuzzy or lumpy, and some have shiny metallic threads in them."

"What kinds of things do you make?"

Alice described the scarves she'd knitted for her family and friends last Christmas. "I can teach you." Her voice rose with excitement. "I can bring my needles and yarn next time I come over..." She caught herself and blushed, her cheeks like red apples.

"Yeah, that would be great. Can you come back next Saturday?"

"Sure! I almost forgot. I have something for you." She grabbed her tote bag and pulled out a large, flat package wrapped in plain brown paper.

"What's this?"

"I know it's a little early for your birthday, but happy birthday, Wendy."

"How nice!" I tore away the wrapping. A book, a hardbound book—but not just any hardbound book. I drank in its beauty and ran my hand over the title: *The Art of Vincent van Gogh.* "Oh, it's wonderful."

"I bought it when we lived in Europe, but I thought you should have it."

"Thank you so much, Alice. I love it." I smiled and hugged the book to my chest, then rested it on my lap. I opened the cover that displayed my favorite painting of all, *Starry Night*. On the inside was printed in block letters:

To Wendy Robichaud

From Alice Frances Rend

A F REND

My jaw dropped open, and I screeched, "Alice! It was you all this time?"

Her kind blue eyes met mine, and she let out a hearty laugh. "I couldn't believe you never figured that out."

I laughed too. "Why didn't you say anything? You wrote *seven* notes!"

Her voice softened. "We didn't really know each other very well. I wasn't sure how you would take it—you know, advice from somebody like me."

I stared at the incredibly thoughtful, smart, and talented person in front of me. All that time I thought I was at the bottom of the heap, Alice thought she was even lower.

"Don't ever worry about that, Alice."

After Alice left, I flipped through the van Gogh book, and my heart warmed all over again at her kindness.

How sad it would've been if I hadn't gotten to know Alice. Not to mention that I probably never would've learned that she wrote the sticky-note messages. We attended the same school for two years but had only a few classes together, other than eighth grade homeroom. I wouldn't have even thought about inviting her to my birthday party this summer.

If Jennifer hadn't left for the summer, if I hadn't searched for someone to fill the void, if...

But I did get to know Alice, because I made it happen. And we became friends quickly. So quickly, it must've broken some kind of record.

My confidence in making new friends went through the roof. Could I achieve the same results anytime, and with anyone?

I analyzed the steps I'd taken with Alice:

1. I paid her a compliment by asking for her help—with paint colors.

2. I invited her to join me somewhere—although it was only my house.

3. I asked a few questions about her life and some topics she was interested in.

4. I let her talk as much as she wanted while I listened.

5. When she offered to do something nice for me, I accepted.

Maybe making new friends didn't come as naturally to me as it did to Jennifer, but I was on to something here. I had accidentally formulated a plan that worked. I sat down at the computer and typed a document with the title:

How to Make Friends in 5 Easy Steps
So Easy Even a Bird Face Can Do It
I would try it again—next time on an adult.

Twenty-six

I visited Dad's house the following Sunday equipped with a customized plan for reaching out to Margaret.

Of course, she was the adult. She should have been the one to make the first move. But I seemed the most uncomfortable, and I was tired of it. Each time I saw Dad, I would see Margaret. That was a given. We'd been forced together like two different-sized pieces of string. Sure, they could be tied into a bow, but like Grand-mere Robichaud used to say, it didn't look pretty or feel right. So I had to try this.

"Hello, Margaret." I gave her my biggest grin.

She blinked like a baby at the exact moment she realizes the doctor is giving her a shot, but right before it makes her cry.

I doubted Margaret ever cried.

"Hel-lo, Wen-dy." She gave Dad a quizzical look.

I wanted to laugh. Instead, I smiled to myself because of a

secret weapon—the best way to get on Margaret's good side. Why didn't I think of it sooner? She loved to cross-stitch. She'd recently finished a complicated landscape scene she was particularly proud of. I figured it would be framed and hanging somewhere in the house by now. Sure enough, there it hung over the fireplace mantle in the family room.

"That looks good." I stood in front of her masterpiece with an index finger pressed against my cheek. "I like the colors and the way they coordinate with the furniture." I really meant that.

Margaret gave me a sideways glance. "Thank you."

At dinner, I casually threw into the conversation that my new friend Alice was going to teach me to knit.

"But I'd love to learn to cross-stitch too." I turned to Margaret. "Would you show me what the back of a cross-stitch piece looks like? Then I think I could figure out how to do it."

Dad, Michael, and Christopher stopped chewing and looked at her too.

"Um, of course." Her fork poised in mid-air. "After dinner."

That night, when Dad and the boys settled down to watch a movie, Margaret took me into the bedroom where she kept her needlework supplies. She brought out everything—from a tray of embroidery threads, neatly arranged in a rainbow of colors, to a file box brimming with patterns for creating cross-stitch pictures.

If she was like I used to be, she needed someone to ask her a question and show an interest in her hobby before she would talk about it. Maybe she felt uncomfortable bringing the subject up herself.

Margaret not only showed me what the back of her current cross-stitch project looked like, but she helped me select a pattern and demonstrated each step in how to cross-stitch.

"This one can be yours." She handed the pattern and supplies to me—the special cloth called aida, some needles, and the thread known as floss in the colors I would need. "Let's find a box so you can take all this home."

It worked! "Thank you, Margaret." I hugged her. "This will be fun."

She smiled. "I'll be happy to help you anytime, if you need me."

At home that evening, I opened the box of cross-stitch supplies. Inside I found an envelope neither of us had put there. It held a letter from Dad.

Dear Wendy,

Although I see you almost every Sunday, there's something I need to tell you, and I feel more comfortable telling you in writing.

I have a problem I've hidden from you for a long time, but I believe you are mature enough now to understand...

Twenty-seven

Dad was an alcoholic.

I stared at the letter written in the chicken-scratch only Mom and I could make sense of. The words blurred in front of my eyes as if two giant hands pressed against the sides of my head and squeezed.

This couldn't be right. Was it some kind of sick joke? I blinked and struggled to focus.

He wanted to tell me now. He thought I could handle it. The drinking started right before he and Mom separated. It took a while for him to get help. One of his friends suggested Alcoholics Anonymous. He was still going through the twelve steps and needed to make amends. *To me.*

A memory broke through the wall of pressure surrounding my head. My tenth birthday. He'd arrived late and without a present. Mom was mad. He'd promised her he'd help with the party. The other kids laughed at him as he stumbled around and talked like an idiot. He ran into the table holding the cake. It slid into the punch bowl, sloshing pink juice on the white tablecloth. The dented cake left chocolate icing on the side of the bowl. I was never so embarrassed in my whole life.

I lifted my eyes from the pages. How could he do that? How could somebody be so stupid? He'd chosen a bottle of booze over *me*? And *Mom*? I closed my eyes and shook my head really hard, then noticed I was gritting my teeth and stopped.

He was sorry he hadn't been a better father, but he was working to improve. Now he had three children. Even more reason to stop drinking. And Margaret was helping him.

Tears streamed down my face. Yeah, sure, *now* you're going to try. What a jerk.

He was late for the Spring Program because he had to meet with his AA sponsor.

Well, wasn't that just too bad, Dad. I crumpled the letter and threw it into the trashcan.

Twenty-eight

I sat on the front porch steps like I had almost every day at the same time since summer started, waiting for the mail. Waiting for Jennifer's first letter to arrive.

As soon as the little white truck pulled up, I sprinted to the mailbox. The mail carrier put a blue envelope into the box.

I grabbed it and ripped it open, then held the letter with trembling hands. In spite of eight states between us, it connected me to Jennifer. A few days before, she'd touched the very paper I touched now. Pastel blue paper with clouds floating across the top, six pages front and back. I held them to my nose. They smelled of jasmine and vanilla.

A real letter—so much better than email. She made it an art form with her silly handwriting, big round, loopy capitals, scratched-out words, lopsided hearts for periods, and everything else that made Jennifer who she was. It was exactly like Jennifer talking to me in person. I pictured her sitting cross-legged in front of me, waving her hands around, her blue eyes wide and sparkling.

Hi, Wendy!

I'm finally here!☺

You wouldn't believe how noisy Manhattan is. Aunt Celeste bought me a pair of earplugs. She said I'd need them to sleep until I got used to the traffic noises at night. I tried them on and the sound inside my ears reminds me of when we listened to that conch shell at the beach.♥

We took a taxi from the airport to the apartment. My first taxi ride!☺ *We passed the tallest buildings I've ever seen. I got dizzy just looking up at them! And people were EVERYWHERE. In all kinds of clothes, some from foreign countries, I guess. But the best were the GORGEOUS outfits on some of the girls. I can't wait to go shopping! You ought to see my aunt's closet—it's stuffed with beautiful clothes. Now you know where I get it from.* ♥

Our building's doorman is the nicest, coolest old guy. He looks like Santa Claus and calls me MISS SAMPSON. He said to let him know if I need anything. I feel so high-class.☺

This evening Aunt Celeste and I walked to the ballet studio. Everybody does a lot of walking around here. The only people I see on bikes are delivery people and couriers running errands. (I'll miss our bike rides together ♥ *) I met my instructor, Madame Marmelle. She has BLUE hair! Crazy! I wanted so bad to laugh but I just swallowed it like we did that time I spiked the pencil* *in Miss Carter's class.* ♥ *Some of the students were hanging around and I met a few. One girl was sort of nice, but the rest acted snooty. There are supposed to be boys here too, but I didn't see any.*

I miss you so much. ♥ *...*

I had to stop. It was like I'd been torn in half, and the best half—Jennifer—was missing. I pressed the open letter against my heart and cried. For me. For being left behind. For what might happen in the future. For the possibility that nothing would ever be the same again.

I collapsed into a wicker chair on the porch and finished reading. I cried again when I went inside and wrote back about my pitiful life without her.

Twenty-nine

Jennifer was the first person I thought of each morning and the last one before I fell asleep. It made my day to check the mail and find one of her letters there, though they were painful to read. Everything about New York was exciting to Jennifer, and with the letters' help, I tried to live the fantastic experiences with her. *Tried*.

Like I'd asked her to, she included some photos, taped to the pages of the second letter. One of herself in Central Park, one at the Empire State Building, and another in front of the Museum of Modern Art, which housed van Gogh's *Starry Night*. She drew arrows pointing to spots in the pictures and wrote hilarious descriptions at angles off to the sides. I laughed until my chest emptied and nothing was left but sadness.

By July, each letter grew shorter. More of a scrawled note than a letter, like an obligation instead of a choice, because she'd made a promise. No smiley faces or hearts or fancy, loopy capitals. But full of excuses. She didn't have much spare time. She practiced five hours a day. She had to get massages for her sore muscles. She needed to prepare special meals to keep her weight down. Her aunt took her out in the evenings to meet people who could advance her future ballet career.

Soon the letters didn't arrive as often, not even once a week. The wait was agonizing. Another twenty four hours before I could check the mail again. *Would there be anything today?*

She was sorry she hadn't written in so long. Some of the other students expected her to hang out with them after class. She could learn so much from them. She hated to say no. Her mother phoned almost every night. What could she do? And other people from home had started writing to her too.

I understood, really I did. It was only natural that the busy life of a ballerina would replace a few old things with new ones. Something—or someone—had to get squeezed out.

Jennifer hinted at making friends with some of the other students. Like Emily from Chicago. The one who wasn't snooty. Was she trying to let me down easy? I had feared when she left that she might make a few new friends. I had to expect that. After all, Jennifer couldn't help being Jennifer.

Then an email came, thanks to her new laptop. With a link to her blog, "Jennifer in New York." Photos with other ballet dancers, arms draped around one another. "Me with Roxie, Lisa, Emily, and Tommy." Jennifer in the middle, laughing. Another with Jennifer seated at an outdoor café with Emily. Jennifer making a face at the camera she held at arm's length, her features distorted as though taken with a phone. *She got a phone? And she didn't call me?*

At first, a tiny jealous pang struck my heart, but the news didn't hurt nearly as much as I thought it would.

Thirty

Alice and I simply had to make the track team on the second try. We'd both blown it the first time, and she still wasn't saying why she'd failed. But I wasn't about to let John-Monster and his big mouth mess this up for me, whether he showed up again or not.

So a few days a week, Alice and I got together to run. Sometimes we ran in my neighborhood and sometimes in hers. If we missed starting out early in the morning, we had to wait until evening. Midday through the afternoon, a wave of heat rose from the road like a sauna.

Lots of times we wanted to skip running altogether. Only nine o'clock in the morning but already so hot. Might rain. Forgot my running shorts. Brought the wrong socks. Goldenrod blooming. Weren't you allergic? But neither of us let the other one whine very long or wiggle out of what we'd agreed to do.

As the summer moved along, it became easier to stick to our plan for another reason—an unexpected one. Mom and Mr. Rend became good friends too, and one of them always drove over to visit the other when Alice or I needed a ride. Actually, they insisted, even when we didn't. Like they needed an excuse to see each other. Alice and I thought that was kind of cute.

Through running and supporting each other, we both became physically stronger and more self-confident. Alice lost twenty pounds, and her acne improved with the help of the lotion I showed her. I grew two inches in height and gained ten pounds, much of it muscle. I stopped using cotton balls to fill out the tops of my dresses. "You are what you are," Alice said.

I took a giant leap—no, not the long jump. Never that. It was something else, and it had nothing to do with the physical body or the fact that I celebrated my fourteenth birthday.

In my mind's eye, I was finally able to draw a portrait of Wendy the young woman, the way I wanted her to be, doing the things I wanted her to do. Not beautiful, not perfect, but unique. Just like the birthday cake I'd drawn in the dark when I was seven.

By the time I responded to Jennifer's second letter, I'd learned how to make as many new friends as I wanted, and one of them was my stepmother. I was involved in lots of new hobbies. Besides running, there was knitting, cross-stitch, and impressionist painting, thanks to inspiration from the van Gogh book. I even helped Mom refinish an old chest of drawers for my room. Who would have thought I'd ever want to do something like that?

I followed through on the commitment Mrs. Villaturo and I made to the animal rescue organization. With my help, Mrs. V fostered her first litter of puppies. We also volunteered to take rescued dogs and cats to visit nursing homes for touch therapy. Alice joined me one Saturday a month to help with Pet Adoption Day.

Never underestimate the power of a woman, I've always said.

Summer days filled my memory as cheerfully as the purple and yellow Louisiana wildflowers growing along the roads where Alice and I ran. I hardly noticed when the letters from Jennifer completely stopped.

Thirty-one

Alice and I followed in silence behind Mom and Mr. Rend, who walked hand-in-hand.

I wore a simple black dress and my first pair of dressy black heels. The bumpy surface of the funeral home parking lot required careful steps. I willed my new shoes not to get scuffed.

"Do you think a person goes to heaven in a case like this?" Mom whispered to Mr. Rend.

"I think only God can know."

They spoke back and forth softly, heads leaning in close together. It was comforting to watch them, a Catholic and a Lutheran, talk about God in a way that was bigger than either of them or their religions.

Mr. Rend pulled the brass handle on one side of a pair of heavy paneled doors. He held the door open, and we filed in. A wave of cool, solemn air flowed over me, and I clutched the collar of my dress to keep the chill from invading my body.

Visitors for the wake filled the foyer wall to wall—classmates, teachers, cafeteria workers, the principal, the custodian. At least a hundred people packed the small space. It overflowed through the doors once we got inside.

Melissa sat on a sofa between two other Sticks. Their eyes were raw, faces puffy. Gayle stood against a wall with another Brainiac. She nodded at me and bit her lower lip.

Mom found the guest book outside Parlor C.

My fingers shook as I picked up the pen and wrote my name. This was my first wake—at least the first one I could remember. All my grandparents except Grand-mere Robichaud had died when I was younger. When Grand-mere died, Mom didn't let me see her body, eaten up with cancer. "Remember her alive and happy."

I returned the pen to its stand and took a deep breath. Better get this over with.

Mom and Mr. Rend passed through the doors of Parlor C ahead of Alice and me. I stepped inside the viewing area and stopped short. Alice ran into the backs of my shoes.

I'd never seen so many flowers. They spilled from the walls to the floor and filled every corner. Their bright colors and sweet fragrances seemed mocking and out of place next to death. Next to John-Monster.

From inside silver picture frames resting on a table nearby, John's image watched me approach his casket. In the eighth-grade class photo of him wearing a dress shirt, tie, and glasses, he dared me to come closer. He smiled, hiding his thoughts, concealing his secret. Next to that image, a younger John stood, holding a reward certificate of some kind. A toddler John laughed from his perch on a shiny tricycle, his hair sticking out on one side. This couldn't be the John-Monster I knew. He looked like my stepbrother Christopher. Funny, sweet, loving.

At any moment, I might faint. I took wobbly steps toward his body. The smells of the flowers made me dizzy, and I dropped to the kneeler in front of the casket just in time, clutching the rail to steady myself.

Because of her many visits to the family counselor's office with her own family, Alice knew John-Monster's parents had sought help for his problems—their family's problems—for a long time. She'd overheard Mr. and Mrs. Wilson describing John's depression to Mr. Rend and telling him that John had tried several times to take his own life.

How she kept those secrets, I'll never understand. "I had to," she said. "I'd want him to do that for me."

In spite of his parents' efforts to get John help, he succeeded in killing himself. The story whispered throughout the funeral home was that his mother had discovered his body, lying in the center of the living room, surrounded by his father's and brother's sports trophies.

Why hadn't anybody at school noticed something was wrong? What about the rest of the Brainiacs—his friends? What about Gayle? What about me?

There were plenty of clues.

John sitting on the edge of the Brainiac group at lunch without talking to anyone.

John trying so hard to be the smartest guy in eighth grade. Acting like he always had to do better than everybody else in class. Looking back, I wasn't the only one he picked on when he did better on a test.

John getting shoved in the hall by an angry Mr. Wilson after he learned John didn't make the track team. Did his father talk to the principal? The high school coaches? Try to pull strings to get him in? John looked humiliated. Apologizing for something he couldn't help. Apologizing for not being like his brother.

It must have been awful for him, feeling like he wasn't good enough. Did John believe his father liked his brother more? Because of sports?

John must have craved to be the best at something, at anything. He even tried to be better at track than me and failed at that too. He tried to mess up other people's chances in order to create a chance for himself. How can a person feel that bad inside?

Maybe John didn't think his father loved him—at all. It stinks when you think that. I should know. What a horrible way to leave this world, thinking that.

I shuddered. There had to be a heaven.

But hadn't Tookie survived? Maybe she figured it all out in time.

John and Tookie—so different on the outside but so much

alike on the inside. Trying to be something they weren't.

I blinked. Weren't they just like I used to be? Behind the masks, behind closed doors, they hurt just like I did. They needed the same thing I needed—to be accepted. *Look at me, this is the real me. I'm worth loving just the way I am.*

The only difference between us was how we tried to get what we needed. And what we did when we failed.

Alice, Mr. Rend, Mom, and I slowly walked back toward Mr. Rend's car.

Mom watched my every move, so I turned her way. "Mom, I just want you to know that I'm not happy John committed suicide."

Her tender eyes crinkled at the corners. She wrapped an arm around me and squeezed. "I didn't think you were, sweetie. You have a bigger heart than that."

"But I wished him dead," I whispered.

She took my hand and we slowed our pace. The Rends walked past us and continued ahead. "That came from your pain. You're not the first person to react that way."

I sighed. "I guess not." Before John wished himself dead, had he wished his father dead? Like I'd wondered if I'd be better off if Dad died?

"Just promise me you'll always talk to me about the things that hurt you." Her voice was a soft blanket surrounding my heart.

I kissed her cheek. "I promise."

And I knew. I knew she knew—about people like me, people like John, people who'd been rejected by someone they loved. Like she'd been.

The Rends waited for us outside the car. Alice held her father's hand, her eyes on me.

I reached for the door handle just as the sun's rays broke through the leaves of some nearby trees. The light reflected on a girl's golden hair.

My heart quickened. I weaved my head from side to side, searching beyond the people scattered between us, until I could see more of the girl, although not her face. She stood against a car a few spaces down, with her back to me, talking to another girl about my age.

"I think that's Jennifer over there." I pointed. "Excuse me a minute, please?"

Mom and Mr. Rend nodded.

I moved as fast as I could on my new heels. Alice trailed behind me.

Let it be her, let it be her. I only needed to hear her voice to know for sure it was Jennifer. Then she waved her hands in the air as she spoke to the other girl, and all doubt disappeared. That same warm and comfortable feeling I had the first day I saw her by the monkey bars returned and filled my chest.

She stood a little taller than I remembered. Her figure had slimmed and become more muscular, but curvier at the same time.

"Jen."

The talking stopped and she turned around. She wore bright red lipstick, but there was no mistaking that grin.

"Wendy!" Then she must have thought about the fact that she was outside a funeral home. She covered her mouth with one hand, but her blue eyes sparkled. She squealed and bounced on her toes.

"How have you been?" I threw my arms around her and hugged her. "When did you get back?"

"Last night." She squeezed me tight. "I was going to call you today, but then I found out about this, and..." Her eyebrows formed an upside-down V.

"That's okay." I nodded. "I understand."

"It's so awful." She shook her head and swallowed. "Who would have thought somebody that smart..."

"I know." I hung my head for a moment. "I keep wondering if we could have done something to help."

Jennifer nodded. "Me too."

I had forgotten Alice, quietly standing at my side. "Oh, I'm sorry—you remember Alice?"

"Sure. Hi, Alice." Jennifer smiled.

"Hi, Jennifer." Alice returned the smile. "Welcome back."

I stared at the girl next to Jennifer, and she stared back at me. I waited for an introduction. None was offered.

"I need to go, but I'll call you tonight, Jen." I squeezed her hand.

"Great," she said. "There's so much I want to tell you."

"Me too." Once again, my eyes were drawn to the girl

standing next to Jennifer. Something familiar about her tugged at my memory.

"How have you been, Wendy?" The girl smiled at me like she really wanted to know.

"Fine, thanks." I tilted my head. Where had I seen her before?

She was about the same height as Jennifer, only not as thin. Short auburn hair framed a round, fair-skinned face that wore little makeup. Friendly brown eyes gazed at me from behind a pair of wire-frame glasses.

The girl laughed. "Don't you remember me?"

She and Jennifer exchanged glances.

I slowly shook my head.

"It's Tookie," Jennifer said.

Thirty-two

"Go, Alice! Go, go!" I yelled through cupped hands.

As if spurred by my command, Alice pumped her legs faster in the 200-meter tryout. She moved with the beauty of a racehorse, dense thigh muscles gliding under her skin, and nostrils flaring. She blasted past a couple of girls and continued around the track in a show of strength. The race ended with Alice a close second behind Gayle, who had made the team last spring.

"Woo-hoo, Alice!" I screamed at the top of my lungs and trotted over to meet her.

"Good job." Gayle patted her on the back. Alice tapped Gayle's arm in return.

A boy handed Alice a towel. She nodded her thanks.

She bent over, hands resting on her knees, as she worked to bring her breathing back to normal. From her bent position, she raised her head and gave me a broad grin, her face brighter than her strawberry-blonde ponytail and drenched in sweat. What a picture that made against the clear blue sky. Someday I'd see one of her like that in the newspaper, I was sure.

I squeezed her shoulder, then offered her a cold bottle of water, which she placed against her forehead. "We're both gonna make it this time."

She nodded again without speaking.

"You're on, Wendy," Coach Caisson said. "Pace yourself so you don't wear out too quickly."

I entered the track with three other freshman girls trying out for the one remaining position for the mile. That's right, the mile. After all, endurance was my thing, wasn't it?

Members of both the girls' and boys' teams dotted the LeMoyne High School track and surrounding field. A scattering of adults sat clustered in the spectator stands.

I took my place on the outside lane and smiled to myself. A butterfly meandered by, in no hurry to get out of the way. He'd soon change his mind. I positioned my left foot against the block, admiring the new pink-and-white track shoes Dad had surprised me with for my birthday. I glanced into the stands, and Dad signaled me with a thumbs-up. Next to him sat Mom and Mr. Rend. They waved and gave me matching smiles.

I shot a grin at all of them, then lowered my head. This was it. I hadn't come this far not to make it. I belonged here.

At the whistle, I pushed off the block. Two other girls sprinted ahead of me.

Let them burn themselves out if they wanted. I concentrated

on my breathing, feeding my muscles the oxygen they needed, as I kept consistent and steady motion.

From the side of the track, Alice waved both arms in the air above her head and shouted, "Lookin' good, Wendy!"

Free. No other word described what it was like for me to run. But I no longer needed to escape anything.

This runner was who I wanted to be. This was what I was meant to do at this moment.

Now it was just me and the track.

I paced myself like Coach Caisson said, conserving my energy until near the end of the third lap. Then I really turned it on, gaining momentum and catching up to the leader. She made the mistake of looking at me as I passed, breaking her rhythm, which helped me even more.

I entered the fourth lap in the lead, my mouth open to take in as much air as possible. I pushed myself to the limit, my legs and lungs burning as though they would tear apart.

The finish line was dead ahead, and it was mine. Dad, Mom, Mr. Rend, Alice, and everybody else screamed their heads off as I surged toward it.

I rocketed across the line first, and Coach Caisson leapt into the air on the other side.

He caught up with me and slapped me on the back after I slowed down. "You're gonna be a record breaker!"

Thirty-three

I lingered inside the car. Clusters of students gathered on the front lawn of LeMoyne High School the first morning of the fall semester.

"Aren't you getting out?" Mom laughed and made a shoo-away motion with her hand.

"Give me a few minutes, if you don't mind." I sighed, doubting whether I was ready, even after looking forward to this day all summer. There'd be faces I recognized but plenty I didn't. Some kids I'd miss and wonder about. And one person—John—wouldn't be found anywhere. If he hadn't killed himself, would we eventually have become friends? I wanted to think so.

Although Jennifer and I remained friends, I now had a new best friend in Alice. If things kept going like they were, she might even become my sister someday. I'd always wanted an older brother, but this might be a better deal. Little Adam would be included. Sort of two-for-one. And Mom might get a second chance at happiness. It would be great for Mom and me to join the Rends and become the kind of family I'd wished for since the divorce. But if that didn't happen, I'd be fine. I'd still have my dad, only better than before. And I'd found the perfect grandmother in Mrs. Villaturo.

My life was good. Not exactly the same one I'd longed for a few months earlier, but it was the life I'd helped create for myself.

I opened the car door. "Thanks for waiting, Mom."

"No problem, sweetie. Have a great day."

I stepped out of the car and closed the door. She pulled onto the street.

"Hi, Wendy." Gayle approached, her movements athletic but cautious. A red knit top set off her brown skin and tucked neatly into the waist of a cute denim skirt. She wore a new hairstyle and a trendy pair of glasses. How pretty her eyes were—glossy cocoa beans set in almond-shaped orbs. I hadn't noticed them before.

"Hi, Gayle," I said, happy to see a familiar face. "How are you?"

"I'm okay." She gave a weak smile, then swallowed. "But I miss John." She turned her face from me, then glanced at me sideways as if expecting a negative reaction.

The way she looked—her sadness—slammed into my chest like a hurricane wind. She faced me again, and her eyes revealed the depth of her loss.

Goosebumps formed on my arms. Had John known she cared so much about him? Would it have made a difference if he had? I reached out and touched her shoulder. *What could I say to console her?* An idea came to me, and I said in a soft voice, "I was thinking—why don't we dedicate our first run to him?"

She searched my face, then nodded. "That would be nice." Tears filled her eyes. "Maybe we can talk about this later, okay?"

"Sure."

She hurried toward the main building.

Good thing she got away when she did, because I would've asked questions maybe too painful to answer. Like, did she regret anything? Did she tell John he was important to her—or was she afraid to?

Please, God, keep me from making that mistake—allowing time to slip by without letting someone I cared about know how I felt.

The bell rang. I shook my head and began to walk.

The late August sun warmed my back, while cool air blowing from the north held a promise of autumn. As I approached the front entrance, the breeze picked up a few fallen leaves from the weathered stone steps. Though not perfect, they were beautiful in their own way. The leaves swirled playfully around my ankles, like Chanceaux's puppies. I smiled.

With eyes cast downward toward the steps, I moved in a daydream of myself on the track, wild and free, my ponytail flowing behind me.

Someone's shoulder bumped against mine.

"Excuse me," a young male voice said.

Startled, I looked up into David Griffin's friendly face.

"I'm sorry, David." I blinked and was back in front of school in a dress and sandals.

He stood there, smiling, and seemed to expect something good to happen from our encounter.

A couple of seconds passed without either of us saying anything.

I drew a deep breath and exhaled. "Well, I guess I'll see you at orientation." I took one step away from him, about to continue on my way.

No, wait—that's what Bird Face would do.

I turned toward him again and returned a smile as big as his. "I really like that shirt you're wearing. The color looks great with your eyes."

The End

Acknowledgments

Heartfelt thanks go to my publisher and executive editor, Chila Woychik, for each sentence and paragraph that was strengthened and made more efficient; and to my content editor, Linda Yezak, for each push to make my main character react and express her emotions more fully. I offer special thanks to Anna O'Brien, who worked with grace and determination to develop a cover reflective of the book's content.

On the personal front, I am very grateful for the selfless advice and encouragement from critique group co-founder T.J. Akers and all our critique group members. In addition, I'd like to express appreciation for authors Fay Lamb, Lee Ann Ward, and Burton Cole, among the first to read the entire manuscript and cheer me on.

Last but not least, I'll be forever grateful to my wonderful husband, Pat, who always believed in me, never let me give up, and taught me that anything is possible.

Made in the USA
Charleston, SC
15 February 2014